# Death's Sweet Song

© 2013
Cover © Elena Elisseeva
Layout by Bryce Pearson


Black Curtain Press
PO Box 632
Floyd VA 24091

ISBN 13: 978-1515426271

First Edition
10 9 8 7 6 5 4 3 2 1

# Death's Sweet Song

**Clifton Adams**

# Chapter One

The blue Buick pulled off the highway about fifty yards past the station. I could see the driver looking back at the cabins, and there was a woman beside him in the front seat. They sat there for two or three minutes while the man made up his mind, and finally the Buick began backing up and stopped in front of the gas pumps.

"Fill her up?" I said.

"All right." He opened the door and got out. "What we're looking for," he said, "is a place to stay for the night. Do you have a vacancy?"

"Sure thing."

There were five cabins behind the station and they were all vacant, Most of them would remain vacant, even during the tourist season. That's the kind of place it was. I wondered about that while I put gas into his car. Here was a tourist with a new car, wearing expensive clothes, so why should he want to put up in a rat trap like mine when there were first-class AAA motels all along the highway?

He must have read my mind.

"Engine trouble," he said. "Nothing serious, but I thought I'd better get a mechanic to look at it."

"Oh. Your best bet is to go back to town and talk to the people at the Buick agency."

He smiled pleasantly. "That's what I was thinking."

He was a pretty good-sized guy, and you could see that he kept in condition. His face was burned to the color of old leather, and I guessed he was the type that spent a lot of time on a golf course, or maybe a tennis court. We talked a little about the weather and how hot it was, and then I hung up the hose and went to work on the windshield. That was when I got my first good look at the woman. And she just about took my breath away.

At first I thought she was asleep. She sat there with her eyes closed, her face completely expressionless. Her hair was blonde and short, and her skin was pale, almost white. She wore tan shorts and a white T shirt. The tan shorts looked almost black against that skin of hers. As I was finishing with the windshield, she opened her eyes. For just an instant we stared at each other through the glass, and then she smiled the smallest smile in the world and curled up slowly like a well-fed cat.

"Will you check the oil?" the man said.

I added a quart of oil. Then we went inside the station and he signed the register: "Mr. & Mrs. Karl Sheldon, St. Louis, Mo."

"You want me to call the Buick agency for you?" I asked.

He smiled again. "Don't bother. I can drive it back to town all right. Anyway, I'd like to freshen up a bit."

I put them in Number 2 cabin, right next to the one I kept for myself. I went around every morning and put the cabins in shape, but it would take more than clean sheets and a few licks with a mop to make them look like anything. They were all just alike, bedroom, bath, kitchenette—lumpy beds, peeling dressers, cracked linoleum on the floors. But I hadn't realized how shabby they really were before I saw the look on that blonde's face.

"Really, Karl! It seems to me—"

"It's just for a little while." And he looked at me, almost apologetically. "Don't bother with the luggage. I'll bring it in after a while."

That was a dismissal, so I went back to the station.

The thermometer on the east side of the wash rack had reached an even hundred. I opened a bottle of Coke and stood in the doorway, watching the endless stream of traffic rushing by on the highway. License tags from everywhere—Nebraska, California, Illinois.... Where do tourists go, anyway, in such a hell of a hurry? What difference does it make? I thought, with a taste of bitterness. They're not going to stop here!

And who could blame them? No air-conditioning, no fancy lunchroom, no AAA sign hanging out. Why *should* anybody want to stop at a place like this?

That started me thinking about Karl Sheldon and that blonde"" wife of his. Now, if I could afford a wife like that, you wouldn't catch me putting up in a fire trap like this, not by a long shot. Sheldon seemed like a nice guy, but apparently he wasn't very smart. A woman like that was meant to have nothing but the best. Several times that afternoon I caught my imagination beginning to get the best of me. That white skin; I'd never seen anything just like it before. I was almost glad when a customer came by and left a flat for me to fix; it gave me something else to think about.

Around five o'clock Ike Abrams, my part-time helper, came on duty, and a few minutes later Sheldon backed his Buick out of the carport and headed toward town.

"I see you've rented one of the cabins," Ike said. "Maybe the tourist business is beginning to hit its stride."

"I hope so. Say, did you notice anything wrong with the way that Buick was running?"

"It sounded fine to me."

Ike may not be the smartest man in the world, but he's as good a shade-tree mechanic as you'll find. When he doesn't hear something wrong with an engine, then there's nothing wrong with it. That started me thinking again. Now, why would Sheldon bother to hand me that cock-and-bull story about car trouble? And even if it was true, why would he wait until five o'clock to get started for a garage that would already be closed for the day?

Well, a man had his own set of reasons for everything, and it was none of my business, anyway. I was just glad that a cabin was rented.

After a while I checked the cash register with Ike, turned the station over to him, and headed toward my own cabin to get cleaned up for my usual date with Beth Langford. I could hear the shower running in Number 2 cabin, and I stopped for a moment and listened, thinking about that blonde. You'd better hold on to that imagination of yours, I thought.

My own cabin was like a farmer's oven at harvest time. The sleazy marquisette curtains hung limp and still at the open windows. No hint of a breeze. Through the sagging screen door I could see the glistening ribbon of Highway 66, and beyond it the shimmering, sun-blasted monotony of Oklahoma prairie. It hurt your eyes, just looking at it.

I tried to tell myself that the tourist business was just getting started, as Ike had said, and pretty soon I'd be renting the cabins every night and the money would begin rolling in.

It was a pipe dream. And I knew it.

I kicked my shoes off and lay across the scorching bed, and in no time at all I was cursing myself for ever getting into the business in the first place. The heat was getting me down. I was going to be late for my date with Beth, but that didn't seem to matter.

For about fifteen minutes I lay there with the sweat rolling over my ribs. Pretty soon that old feeling of frustration began gnawing at me, that nameless anger that I knew so well began sinking its claws in my guts.

I wondered if Karl Sheldon appreciated the woman he had. I wondered if he appreciated that car of his, the money in his wallet, the way he could afford to live. By God, I thought, I would appreciate them if I had them!

There had been a time when I was going to have such things. There had been a time when I was going to take the world apart and put it together again just the way I wanted it.

But it didn't work out like that. Nothing worked out the way I planned it. Even now I could feel this tourist-court business falling down around my shoulders. Another failure, Hooper; but you ought to be used to it by now.

I never got used to it. Every time I went under, something inside me got harder, that anger got hotter. One of these days, I thought, I'm going to do it!

But not today.

I lay there, groggy and listless in the heat, "not caring a damn whether or not I ever got up, whether I ever kept my date with Beth Langford. Finally I did get up and stripped and got under the shower. The cold water jarred me, made me feel a little better. I pulled on some clean slacks and a fresh shirt and got out of that cabin before the heat could get another hold on me. Mrs. Sheldon was sitting on the steps of Number 2.

"Is it always this hot in Oklahoma?" she said.

"In July it is. It usually cools off, though, when the sun goes down."

She shrugged faintly, as though she didn't believe me. A white pique skirt-and-halter outfit had taken over for the shorts and T shirt, but the effect was about the same. Sitting in front of that cabin, she looked crisp and fresh, as out of place as caviar in an Army mess kit.

"This is quite a place you have here," she said dryly. "Do you own it?"

"Me and the bank."

She smiled. It was an expression that came slowly, and you didn't realize that it was there at all until it hit you. Then she stretched those white legs out in front of her and lay back with her elbows on the top step. I must have been staring pretty hard, but she didn't seem to notice.

"Were you ever a fighter?" she asked.

It seemed like a funny question. "I was never a boxer, if that's what you mean."

"You've got the build for it."

I didn't know what to say to that. It made me uncomfortable, the way she looked at me, and I wondered if she was laughing at me. About that time I saw Sheldon's Buick turn off the highway and decided it was time I got away from there.

When I got back to the station I saw that Ike had washed down the driveway and swept the office—things I never remembered to do. "If I'm not back by ten o'clock," I said, "go ahead and lock up." I left my keys with him, then got into my '47 Chevy and headed for town.


When you take 66 into Creston, your first impression is that it's a pretty good-sized place. The first things you see are the oil-well supply houses, big sprawling buildings and sheds, long rows of powerful cementing trucks, pumpers, testing and drilling equipment. Acres of buildings and acres of trucks, millions of dollars' worth of equipment. It's pretty impressive the first time you see it.

Right next to the railroad are the grain elevators, great towering cement columns standing solid and proud like lonesome skyscrapers in the middle of the prairie. And then there's the big overpass at the railroad. You cross the overpass and drop down on the other side and you're in Creston.

You take one look at the town and feel cheated.

You'd been led to expect great things and here you are right in the middle of another one-horse prairie town. I'd lived here all my life, knocking out four years in the Army, and I never failed to be disappointed when I looked at it. It was a fairly clean town, as prairie towns go, once you moved away from the cluster of produce and feed companies that huddled around the grain elevators. Coming down the town side of the overpass, you could see it all. The straight, treeless streets. The frame houses and parched lawns. The new, raw-looking high school, the cement tennis courts, the white afterthought of a steeple on the Baptist church.

It was my home. A place where eight thousand people, more or less, lived, loved, hated, worshiped, spawned. I knew everybody and everybody knew me, and that's the kind of arrangement you can get pretty sick of after a while.

For a minute I thought I'd drive around to the family house and say hello to my dad, but I stopped at a drive-in instead and had a beer. At that moment, with the bank breathing on my neck, I didn't feel up to lying about how good business was and how much money I was making. And I didn't want Dad asking if Beth Langford and I had set the date yet. He didn't know it, and Beth didn't know it, but there wasn't going to be any date. That's one thing I was sure of.

The carhop, the sister of a guy I had known in high school, brought me the beer.

"How's the tourist business, Joe?"—"Fine. Just fine."

What a joke! I thought. They always asked the same question and I always gave the same answer, lying in my teeth. But, at times like this, there was always one comforting thought in the back of my mind—this tourist business was purely a temporary arrangement. A breather, a stopover on the way to something big.

If they thought I was going to stay bogged down in Creston the rest of my life, they were crazy. There was a limit to the number of craps a man could throw, no matter how unlucky he was. Sooner or later his luck had to change, and I could feel it in my bones that my turn was about to come up.

I had a theory about this business of getting ahead in the world. Once, at least once, in every man's life there comes a chance to make a killing, a chance to lift himself out of the dung heap. I'd seen it happen too many times. I'd seen oil-field roughnecks become millionaires, betting their hard-earned cash on good structures that the big companies had missed on. I'd seen two-bit land men become big shots overnight.

There is no mystery about how one man gets to be a big shot while the man right beside him remains a bum all his life. One man saw the once-in-a-lifetime opportunity when it appeared, recognized it for what it was, grabbed it.

There's no mystery about it at all. The only two requirements are plenty of patience and a world of guts. And this is the way it works:

Herb Carter was a small-time land man for a big-time oil company. His job was to go out and lease up land that the company wanted, land that had been proved either by existing producing wells, or by geophysical exploration—proved at a cost of maybe a million dollars to the company. It happened that Herb had a friend who was the chief engineer for an exploration company, and this was the once-in-a-lifetime opportunity that Herb didn't miss. From his friend Herb got the exact location of the prize structure and leased the land for himself.

It sounds pretty simple, but it took plenty of guts. Herb Carter had blackballed himself for life, he had practically robbed his company of a million dollars that they had sunk into the exploration of that land. But he took the chance. He let the company scream. He fought off lawyers and began to drill.

Now, there is just one way in God's world to tell you if a structure will produce oil, and that is to sink a hole. They can shoot the land a thousand times and locate faults, salt domes, anticlines, any of which might produce oil, but the only way to tell is to sink a hole. And every time you sink a hole the odds are nine to one that it will be dry. Herb knew this before he started, but he also knew that this was his one chance, his only chance, to hit the top, so he let them scream and he drilled.

It happens that Herb hit it to the tune of five million, and I had heard the story all my life. But the lesson in the story is not that he hit; the lesson is that he had the guts to recognize an opportunity and grab it.

Herb Carter's story was one I never forgot, and its lesson stuck with me. Have patience, have faith, and have the guts when the time comes to act. So when they asked me about the tourist business I could look them in the eye and say: "Fine. Just fine." Because I knew that one day my turn would come.

I tramped the horn and had the carhop bring me another beer, knowing that I was going to be late, knowing that Beth didn't like the smell of beer on my breath anyway, and not caring somehow. I was thinking about that blonde out at the tourist court.

Now, there is a woman, I thought, that a man could get excited about. If I was on my way to pick up a woman like that, you wouldn't find me killing time in a drive-in. You could bet your life on that!

But habit had its way, finally. I settled the tab with the girl and headed the Chevy toward town.

The Langford place was on Third Street, a one-story white frame house right across from the Methodist church, where Beth and I used to go to Sunday school, and where Beth still did. The house had been standing there ever since I could remember, just like my own family place a block away, and it never seemed to change. It got a fresh coat of white paint every other spring, the hedge was always neatly trimmed, the lawn always mowed.

It was a lot like our own place, except that Mr. Langford was not a doctor, like my dad, and had more time to keep the place in shape. It was seven-thirty when I pulled the Chevy into the driveway, almost dark, and Old Man Langford had just finished watering the front lawn.

"You're late tonight, aren't you, Joe?"

Be thirty minutes late for a date and the whole town knew it; that's the way Creston was. "I got held up at the station," I said. "I thought maybe we'd have a sandwich and see a movie. There's plenty of time for that."

"Sure," Langford said doubtfully, then shrugged. "How's the tourist business?"

"Fine. Just fine."

But I wasn't fooling him one little bit. If business was so fine, I'd be driving a better car. Langford was a retired real-estate man and he knew the signs. Then the front door opened and Beth came out.

"I'm sorry I'm late," I said, hardly seeing her.

I'd seen her so many times, had had so many dates with her exactly like this one, that there was nothing fresh or new about it. Long ago I had slipped into the habit of taking Beth for granted. I knew just about everything there was to be known about her; I could guess beforehand just what she would wear, what she would say, how she would react to any given situation.

I could look at her as I was doing now, and never actually see her, because I knew her as well as I knew my right hand, and a man doesn't have to keep looking at his hand to make sure it hasn't changed.

"A sandwich and a movie?" I asked.

She smiled and I knew the exact words she would answer with. "Sure, Joe. A sandwich and movie sounds nice."

There was a drive-in movie on the highway south of town, and that's where we went. But I couldn't tell you what the picture was about. I don't remember her name, but the girl in the picture was blonde and plenty good-looking, and the husky way she had of talking kept reminding me of that girl back at the tourist court, that Mrs. Sheldon.

I kept remembering the funny way she had looked at me, and that remark she had made about my build.

"What is it, Joe?"

"What?"

"I thought you had gone to sleep," Beth said.

I became aware of the giant screen in front of us. "I wasn't asleep," I said. "I was thinking."

"I thought you liked John Wayne. If you want to go, Joe, it's all right with me."

"I like John Wayne fine. Let's watch the picture."

She looked puzzled. Then, almost immediately, she slipped back into that Hollywood dream. I looked at her and had the uneasy feeling that I was sitting beside a total stranger. I looked at her objectively, the way you would look at a photograph of a person you had never seen. By no stretch of the imagination could she be called beautiful, or even pretty, although she was pleasant enough to look at, and certainly she wasn't ugly.

Her face was small, and her hair was rather thick and long, which was the wrong way to wear it. Even I knew that. Her figure was all right, if a little thin. But her arms always freckled in the summer, and they were freckled now. Her eyes, I think, were the best part of her. They were large and startlingly clear.

It's difficult to dislike people with eyes like Beth's, and maybe that's the reason I had fallen into the habit of dating her. But what the hell, I thought. A guy had to do something. If she had let herself believe that it meant something, it wasn't my fault.

She turned her head briefly and looked at me. She smiled and took my hand and squeezed it. The night was hot and her palm was sweaty, and I had to go through an elaborate act of lighting a cigarette to get my hand free. My nerves were beginning to get on edge and I didn't know exactly why.

I settled back in the seat, tried to get comfortable, and stared determinedly at the screen.

It wasn't a minute before I was thinking of that blonde again.

## Chapter Two

I went straight back to the station after taking Beth home. The place was dark; Ike Abrams had already called it a day and locked up. I put the Chevy in the carport and then went around and checked all the locks to see that Ike hadn't missed anything. Four of the cabins were still empty, I noticed. Right at the height of the tourist season and only one cabin rented!

The dead, hot air hit me in the face as I went inside my own shack. The lights were still on in the Sheldon cabin, and I could hear the muffled sounds of their talking, without being able to understand what they were saying. Probably, I thought, that blonde is still raising hell about having to stay in such a place.

Well, I couldn't blame her for that.

Think about something else, I thought. Or think about nothing—that's better. Just get your clothes off and hope a breeze comes up and you'll be able to get some sleep before the sun comes up again.

It wasn't any good. The bed was hot, and pretty soon it was clammy with sweat, and I lay there in the darkness smoking cigarettes and wondering when the hell my luck was going to change. When would I be able to pull out of this hole for good?

Times like this were the toughest. It isn't easy to have faith when you're alone. The harder you pray for a break, the more they seem to avoid you, and pretty soon you begin thinking that maybe you've got it figured all wrong, that maybe you're destined to be stuck here the rest of your life, just, the way you are now.

That's when it gets tough, when you have no money, when you have no special influence, and you know there's no way in the world to go out and make something happen. All you can do is wait and be ready to take advantage of any break that happens to come your way—but they never seem to come. And soon, if you let yourself, you'll get to believe they'll never come.

When I'd got out of the Army I'd gone to work in the Provo Box Factory in Creston—just marking time, I told myself. I'll keep my eyes open and wait for something to come up. Then there had been rumors of a big superhighway project along Route 66 and I had grabbed this tourist court on a GI loan. The superhighway project had flopped, and with it my plans for big right-of-way profits. So I was right back where I'd started, except that I was now saddled with a slipping business.

It was almost midnight and not getting any cooler. Disgusted, I got out of bed and walked around in my shorts. Then I thought: Hell, I might as well go outside if I want to walk. So I put on my pants and a pair of moccasins and went outside.

The lights were still on in Number 2, and they were still talking. That Sheldon! Why didn't he just get in that Buick of his and start driving? That's what I would do if I was in his shoes.

I sat on the steps arid started to light another cigarette. But something stopped me. I didn't know what it was at first, but I knew something wasn't right. I listened hard, the unlighted cigarette in my mouth, but the only thing I could hear was the talking over in Number 2. Sheldon and his wife. I listened some more, knowing that something was wrong, but I couldn't put my finger on it.

Then it hit me. It wasn't Sheldon and his wife talking; it was Sheldon and another man!

I couldn't hear what they were saying, but the talk kept going on and on between the men, and only occasionally did Mrs. Sheldon put in a word. The thing seemed funny to me. If Sheldon knew anybody in Creston, he hadn't mentioned It. Then I remembered that car trouble that didn't seem to exist. And the fact that he had chosen one of my shacks instead of a first-class motel. And now he was receiving company at midnight, in a place where he was supposed to be a stranger.

Little things, but put them together and it came to a pretty queer situation.

I had no qualms about eavesdropping; I was trying to hear what they were saying now, but the words were mushy and senseless by the time they had drifted over to where I was. Finally I got up and swung wide around the carport and came up in the shadows by the east window. You're going to have a hell of a time explaining this, I told myself, if Sheldon happens to look out that window and sees you standing here.

I needn't have worried. The shades were drawn, the windows and door were closed. With no ventilation, the thermometer inside that cabin must have been reaching for 105, and that only made me more curious. What could be so important that a man would take precautions like that?

I stood there behind the carport for maybe three or four minutes before anything began to make sense, and then I heard Sheldon saying:

"It sounds too good. That's the trouble. I don't like jobs that look like pushovers, because there isn't any such thing."

"Just the same," the other man said, "this one is a pushover. I tell you I would have done it myself, all alone, if it hadn't been for that safe."

"Prisons are full of men who thought a job was a pushover. Well, let me see that sketch again."

Then, after a few seconds of silence, "Look. From this first-floor window to the front office, how far is it?"

"I don't know. Forty, fifty feet, I guess."

"I want to know exactly how far it is, right down to the last inch," Sheldon said. "It's going to be dark and we're not going to have a guide to lead us by the hand. I want every piece of furniture listed, in the storeroom as well as in the office, and I want all the electrical wiring checked. That's very important. How about burglar alarms?"

The other man laughed. "Not a chance."

"I know a hundred men who said the same thing," Sheldon said dryly. "They're in cells now."

"Cripes, I can't go in there with a yardstick and measure the place off for you. I'm takin' a big chance as it is."

"All right," Sheldon said flatly, "we'll forget the whole thing. The deal's off. I told you how I work, and that's the way it's got to be."

For several minutes they just haggled, Sheldon saying the deal was off and the other man trying to change his mind. I stood there thinking: Well, I'll be damned! It didn't take a mindreader to figure out what they were planning. They were planning to rob somebody! That realization stunned me for a moment, and I guess a kind of panic took hold of me. This was a hell of a thing. The only thing I could think of was getting to a telephone and calling the Creston County sheriff.

But that would be foolish. What could I tell him? I didn't know who they were planning to rob, or how, or when, or anything else. The only thing to do was wait and see if I could learn something else.

So I waited. They were still haggling about how it ought to be done. After a while I stopped listening to what they were saying and began concentrating on the man Sheldon was arguing with. The voice sounded vaguely familiar. I couldn't pin it down exactly, but there was one thing I would bet on: He was a native of Creston. The thing that puzzled me was how a native of Creston ever got to know a man like Sheldon.

"Now, wait a minute. Maybe a hundred and fifty people work at this factory. They draw between fifty and a hundred and fifty a week, so what does that make a two-week payroll? Close to thirty thousand dollars, the way I figure it. Think of it! Are you sayin' we should forget thirty grand?"

"I'm saying the job will be done my way or not at all."

"All right, all right! I'll get the information you want. I don't know how I'll do it, but I'll do it. Now is everything all right?"

"Everything is just fine," Sheldon said pleasantly. "Now let's have another look at that sketch. Did you notice what kind of safe it is?" .

"All I know is that it's big and looks plenty rugged."

"Get me the make and model and it won't be so rugged. Now tell me about this factory again; I want to hear everything there is to know about it."

I already knew what factory it was, because there was only one factory in Creston, and that was the one that made boxes. It was owned by a tough old Bohunk named Max Provo, and I had worked there one summer after getting out of the Army. I had sweated off fourteen pounds in the place for a lousy fifty bucks a week. I'd never thought of it before now, but it was a wonder the place hadn't been robbed long ago, considering how it was run.

Old Provo was the kind of penny-pinching gaffer who never put out a dollar if he didn't absolutely have to. Long ago he had figured out that writing checks cost money. A hundred pay checks, costing about ten cents each, meant that he would have to pay out ten dollars every two weeks for nothing. Twenty dollars every month, two hundred and forty every year. Not for a man like Provo. He paid in cash.

And did he have the cash brought out in an armored car?

Not Provo; that kind of foolishness cost money. He picked up the cash himself and made the bank furnish armed guards, free of charge. And he picked the cash up the day before payday and made the office force come in an hour early the next morning in order to get the payroll ready by noon. That was Provo's idea of good business, squeezing that extra hour's work out of the office force.

Well, by God! I thought. At that moment I was remembering the long hours and low wages and bad working conditions, and I was almost ready to go back to my cabin and forget that I had heard anything. Let them take the cheap bastard. Let them take him good; it was none of my business, anyway.

I don't know—if I had walked off right then, maybe that's just the way it would have happened.

But I didn't walk off. I heard Sheldon saying: "Now about the watchman; what kind of routine does he follow?"

The other man laughed shortly. "His routine is to sit in the garage arid read Western magazines. He's about sixty years old, he's got a gimpy leg, and on top of that he's half deaf. You could probably blow the safe with him right there in the garage, and he'd never even know about it."

I got the unpleasant feeling that Sheldon was not amused. "He'll have to be taken care of," he said flatly, "but that shouldn't be any trouble. Now look. Here's a list of things I want you to do. Today's the seventh, isn't it? Yes, the seventh. Paula and I will leave this place first thing in the morning, and we'll come back on the fourteenth. I'll pick up the things I need and we'll take care of that safe the night of the fourteenth. That's right, isn't it?"

The other man must have nodded. "All right," Sheldon said, "that's all there is to it. We'll come back to this same place. It's a lousy place, but there's one thing about it—it isn't crowded with tourists who might recognize me. The farmer that runs the place is too stupid to guess anything. He'll think we're just returning from our vacation."

The other man sounded amused. "It's funny, in a way. Joe Hooper used to work at this factory."

"Who's Joe Hooper?"

"The guy that owns this fly trap you're stayin' in."

The meeting was about to break up. Paula Sheldon began

complaining about the heat and somebody opened the window, but not until I was well back in the shadows.

Stupid farmer! I thought. Well, by God, we'll see about that! You're going to look pretty silly, Sheldon, when you tackle that safe with a roomful of deputy sheriffs looking on!

I got back to my cabin just in time. I saw the lights go out in Number 2, then the door opened and a man came down the steps. He came right in front of my cabin, whistling softly through his teeth, and suddenly I had him pegged. His name was Bunt Manley. He was a thickset bull of a man, wearing a flapping sport shirt and a wide-brimmed straw sombrero. He walked around the far side of the station, and after a while I heard a car pull off toward Creston.

Well, I thought, the picture is beginning to fall in place. I didn't know Bunt Manley very well, but I knew that he had recently served a year and a day in Leavenworth for some dealings in moonshine whisky, and that was probably where he had met Sheldon.

I lay across the bed again and pieced the thing together as well as I could. It was possible that the robbery had been Sheldon's idea in the first place, but it didn't seem likely to me. Probably Manley had spotted the box factory as a soft touch and had got in touch with Sheldon, who seemed to consider himself an expert on safes.

Looking at it objectively, I had to admit that they were . working it very nicely. Almost every man in Creston had worked in the box factory at one time or other, and probably Bunt Manley had too. So he would know the place, and there would be no special reason to suspect that he had a hand in the robbery. Sheldon, of course, was just a man on a vacation. You couldn't arrest a man and his wife for spending the night in a tourist court.

It was a nice setup, with one exception. I knew about it.

Tomorrow, I thought, the Sheriff will know about it. Comes the night of the fourteenth and we'll see who's the stupid farmer, Mr. Sheldon!

I couldn't sleep. This new excitement had me alive to my fingertips and I was up pacing the floor all over again. What a hell of a thing this is! I thought. Planning a robbery right here in one of my own cabins—a thirty-thousand-dollar robbery! The thought of so much money stunned me. Thirty thousand dollars, just for one night's work!

Of course, there was going to be a monkey wrench in Sheldon's machinery, and I was going to throw it. But the idea that the thing could be done, if it weren't for me, just about knocked the breath out of me. All that money!

Hooper, I thought, what could you do with that much money? Think of it!

I didn't dare think of it. Sure, I was looking for a break, an angle to grab hold of, but this business of pulling a robbery was too much of a gamble. No, sir, a thing like this just wasn't in my line.

But it was a pile of money, more money than I had ever had at one time, and it was hard getting my mind on anything else. Across the way the lights were still on in Number 2. The door was open now and I could see Sheldon working over some papers at the table. I didn't see the blonde.

Then I did see her. She was outside, sitting on the bottom step of the cabin, and the slant of light from the doorway just fell across the top of that platinum hair. I sat on the edge of the bed for a long while, just watching her, and it was then that I realized that she had hardly been out of my mind from the first moment I'd seen her. All afternoon she had moved back and forth through my consciousness. Even tonight, when I'd been with Beth, she had been in my brain.

Well, I thought, you might as well forget her, Hooper, because in just one more week she's going to be in jail, along with Sheldon and Manley. I wondered what Sheldon was doing there at the table—probably going over those sketches that Manley had made of the factory.

As I watched, the blonde stood up and stretched, and then she called, "How much longer are you going to be, Karl?"

"Not long," Sheldon said. "Why don't you go to bed?"

"I can't sleep with the lights on. Besides, it's too hot."

Sheldon said something else and his wife stood there for a moment, smoothing down her hair. Then she turned and started walking out toward the highway—not going anywhere, just walking to kill time while her husband got caught up on his homework. If I had a wife like that, I thought, I wouldn't be fooling with paperwork this time of night; you could bet on that!

But when you're a professional safecracker, I guess you have to work odd hours. I turned around and watched the blonde go past my door, and then I went to the door and watched her walk as far as the station. She didn't do anything. She just stood there and looked at the empty highway, and you could almost tell how bored she was by the way she stood. I lit a cigarette and told myself it was time to get some sleep.

I didn't budge.

As long as she was where I could see her, I couldn't take my eyes off her. After a while she moved around to the other side of the station, making a wide, lazy circle on her way back to the cabin. I went to the icebox to get myself a beer, and when I got back to the door she was standing right there at the bottom step.

She laughed softly, and just the sound of her voice was enough to shake me.

"I saw your cigarette," she said. "The heat keeping you awake too, Mr. Hooper?"

For a moment it was pretty awkward. I couldn't think of anything to say. She had known all along that I had been watching her and it didn't seem to bother her a bit.

Then a cloud slid from under the moon and there was sudden light in front of my cabin. I saw that she was smiling. "Is that beer you're drinking?" she asked.

"There's more in the icebox, if you'd like one."

"I think that would be fine," she said softly, still smiling.

I had a fast pulse as I went for the beer. I kept reminding myself that it was all probably very innocent, that she was just bored and wanted to talk. Still, that was the way things got started.

I didn't have any definite plans; I'd just take her the beer and see where we went from there, if anywhere. When I stepped out of the kitchen I saw that she was no longer outside by the steps.

She was there in my room.

Well, I thought, that's laying it on the line where you can't miss it! She was standing there with an unlighted cigarette in her fingers, and I must have set the beer down somewhere because I didn't have it when I stepped over and held a match for her. For a moment neither of us did anything. We just stood there looking at each other getting the situation down pat. Then I grabbed for her.

She slipped out of my arms like a greased cat. "Are you always so impulsive, Mr. Hooper?"

"That's the way I am, I guess. And the name's Joe."

"And I'm Paula." She smiled. "Now do I get that beer?"

That was when I began to burn. I felt like the guy who had the wallet pulled away from him just as he was about to pick it up. But I got the beer. I found the can on the kitchen table and gave it to her.

"Now you're mad," she said, still smiling.

I said nothing.

She drank some of the beer and put the can down. "Does it always have to mean the same thing," she asked, "when a girl steps into a man's room?"

"Am I making a beef?"

"No. But you're mad; it shows all over."

I was mad, all right, but not nearly so much as I had been at first. Nothing had really changed. She hadn't turned indignant or tried to slap me, so I knew that nothing had changed but the timing. And I could change my timing. For a Paula Sheldon I could change a lot of things.

"All right," I said, "maybe I'm mad, but I'll get over it. Do you want another beer?"

"No, I'd rather talk."

"All right. What do we talk about?"

Still smiling, she hit me with it. "Let's talk about what you heard at our window tonight."

I couldn't have been more stunned if she had fired a pistol in my face. I stood like a post as she stepped around the bed, looked once through the window to make sure that her husband was still busy with his paperwork, then pulled the shade. She wasn't smiling now. She meant business.

"How much did you hear, Joe?" she said.

I shrugged as if to say I didn't know what she was talking about.

"You heard enough," she said. "I was on the bed when Karl and Manley were talking. You couldn't see me, but I could see you through the gap between the window shade and the facing."

There was nothing I could say to that. She had seen me.

What got me was why she hadn't yelled at the time, giving Manley and Sheldon a warning.

She knew what I was thinking.

"You're wondering why I kept quiet about it," she said. "I did it because this job has to go through. There can't be any backing out, because Karl has to have the money. Do you have any idea how many strings have to be pulled to get a man out of prison? It took almost ten thousand dollars to get Karl a parole, and now the string pullers want to be paid, or they'll send him back faster than they got him out. If he's lucky."

I hardly heard what she was saying. She had moved closer, pressing against me, and then those white arms crawled around my neck and she turned her face up to me.

"Do you understand, Joe?"

The only thing I understood was the excitement that took hold of me when she touched me, as the softness of her seemed to melt against me, as I tried to capture that red mouth that kept slipping from one side to the other.

"Joe, do you understand what you must do?"

"I understand."

She was a fire inside me, spreading through me, racing like flame. She was still talking as I forced her back. I tightened my arm around her, bowing her back, bending her knees, and suddenly both of us came crashing down on the bed. She was still talking. "Joe, nothing must happen to stop this factory job! No one must know about it! No one!"

"I said I understood."

"Promise, Joe, that you'll tell no one!"

"Great God, what do I have to say to convince you? All right, I promise!"

Only then did she stop squirming and fighting, only then did I capture that red mouth of hers. Her arms tightened around my neck in the kind of nervous excitement that is impossible to fake. Her dagger-sharp nails gouged into my shoulders as she pulled me down with her, then she took my hand in hers and guided it, and for a long while there was no sound in the room except that of our breathing.

"Joe..."

I wasn't sure how much time had passed. The bright, "clean fire was dead, and the stifling heat of the Oklahoma summer moved into the room.

"Joe..."

I said nothing. The thing to watch about climbing so high is the terrible fall to the ground. I laughed.

"Joe, what is it?"

"Nothing."

I had no wish to touch her or look at her or anything else. After a while she got up and went to the window, again, and I guess Karl Sheldon was still busy with his burglary plans, because Paula seemed in no hurry to leave. She came back and sat on the edge of the bed.

"Joe, you meant it, didn't you? You won't do anything that might affect our plans?"

I looked at her then, amazed that she looked exactly the same as she had before—completely unruffled, as pale as the moon. Even then, at a time like that, with the heat in the room so heavy that it was almost impossible to breathe, all I had to do was look at her and that sure excitement began to take hold again. Instinctively I reached out for her, but she laughed softly and moved away.

She was waiting for an answer, for some assurance that I was going to keep my promise. I wasn't even sure what it was I had promised. I made another grab and she slithered away again, and this time she stood up and moved into the deep shadows on the other side of the room. It was almost as though a powerful field of magnetic attraction had been removed. Now that I could hardly see her, I could think again.

"Well..." she said. Not impatiently, not uncertainly. It was just an invitation to get on with the particular business at hand.

"I gave you my word," I said. "I won't break up your husband's plans."

Like hell I wouldn't break up his plans! What if something got fouled up and something went wrong with the robbery? Where would that put me? I knew where it would put me, if it ever came out that I had known about the robbery beforehand. It would put me in a cell right alongside Sheldon and Manley. Accessory before the fact— I wasn't so stupid that I didn't know what that meant.

I sat up and lit a cigarette to give my hands something to do while I thought it out. She was a hell of a woman, there was no doubt about it....

"I know what you're thinking," she said, almost gently, and I imagined that I could hear that faint half-smile in her voice.

"Do you?"

"You were wondering if the payment was right for the job."

"I was wondering what your husband would do if he knew I had listened in tonight."

"That's easy," she said. "He simply wouldn't go through with the job. That's how he is. If a thing isn't set up perfectly, he doesn't touch it."

"And if he doesn't go through with this one, he goes back to prison?"

She nodded. "Or worse."

I found an ash tray and mashed out the cigarette.

"You know," I said, "this thing could be as dangerous for you as it is for your husband. You must love him very much, coming here like this...."

Nothing at all flustered her. She laughed. "As a matter of fact, I don't love him at all." And she had already anticipated the next question. "Then why am I married to him? Maybe I'll tell you someday."

She moved out of the shadows then and came across the room again. This time she didn't slip away when I reached for her. For just a moment the hard fire raged and she gouged her fingers into my shoulders as I kissed her.

"I like you, Joe!" The words came through her teeth, hissing.

Then she was gone. Holding her when she didn't want to be held was like trying to squeeze moonlight in your hands. She was out of my arms and out of the cabin before I could stop her. There was nothing I could do about it.

There was little sleep for me that night. My nerves were strung as tight as cat gut on a violin.

After a while the light went out in the Sheldon cabin and the night was completely quiet. There was not a breath of breeze to move the limp curtains, to relieve the heat. When I looked hard into the shadows I could almost see her standing there. I could reach out and almost touch her. And all I could do was lie there and sweat, giving myself plenty of good advice that I knew I wasn't going to take.

But all things end, if you wait long enough, and finally that night ended. I opened the station as usual around seven o'clock, and about thirty minutes later Karl Sheldon and Paula came around in the Buick.

I lifted my hand when Sheldon waved. "We're going down to Texas to see my wife's people," he called. "On our way back we may be stopping with you again."

"I'll be looking for you."

Paula didn't even look at me. Which was just as well.

As the Buick pulled onto the highway and slipped into the stream of early-morning traffic, panic took hold of me. Christ! I thought. How are you going to explain this to the Sheriff, Hooper? What are you going to say when he asks why you stood here and let them drive away?

Then I thought: Now, wait a minute. There's nothing to get panicky about, because, as far as you know, they haven't done a damn thing that they could be arrested for. All they've done is talk. And there was no way in the world I could prove that.

Sure, I thought. That makes sense. The robbery doesn't take place for another seven days, so just phone the Sheriff and tell him what you know.

I didn't do it.

The first thing I knew, it was noon, and I still hadn't done anything about calling the Sheriff. Something seemed to happen every time I started to call. First it was a farmer wanting coal oil, then a flat to fix, then a lube job, and then the morning was gone. Once I had been putting gas in a car, and the driver got out and said, "What the hell do you think you're doing?" The tank had overflowed and gas had gone over his rear fender and was splashing onto the driveway. "What are you thinking about, anyway?"

I could have told him, but I didn't. I had been thinking about that blonde wife of Sheldon's.

That threw a scare into me. Well, by God! I thought. Are you still remembering that little blonde tramp, Hooper. Is it because of that promise to her that you can't find time to call the Sheriff's office?

Oh, she's quite a woman, all right, that Paula Sheldon, but you'd better be sensible about this thing, Hooper, or you're going to have more trouble than you can handle!

Paula, I thought, you're going to look like hell in one of those prison dresses, but there's not a thing I can do about it. I quit the lube job I'd been working on, went into the station, and picked up the phone. After a minute a voice said, "Sheriff's office, King speaking."

"Ray, this is Joe Hooper. Let me speak to the Sheriff, will you?"

"The Sheriff just left for lunch. Anything I can help you with, Joe?"

"No. Thanks, anyway. It's nothing important." Suddenly I was glad the Sheriff wasn't in, because the thing was too involved to tell over the phone. When Ike came on duty, I'd go down to the office and talk to him. That was what I told myself.

"By the way," the deputy said, "how's the tourist business, Joe? They keepin' you pretty busy out there?"

"Yes, pretty busy. Well, see you around, Ray."

I hung up and looked at my hands. They were shaking. I felt like the man who walked away from a head-on collision.

What's the matter with you, Hooper, have you lost your mind completely?

I knew what was the matter with me. I was beginning to get an idea. It came with a rush, and suddenly it stood there full grown, grinning at me. This is the way, it said.

This is how it's going to be!

# Chapter Three

About two o'clock that afternoon the Sheriff called.

"Joe, this is Otis Miller. Ray King said you called while I was out to lunch. Anything I can do for you?"

"Yes," I said. "I talked to Ray, and maybe I should have told him about it, but I decided to wait until I could see you. I'm afraid I got suckered, Sheriff. I was going through my cash drawer this morning and found a five-dollar bill that looks like it was printed on newsprint."

"Counterfeit?"

"Queer as a thirty-cent piece. I don't know why I didn't notice it before. Too busy to pay attention, I guess."

"Well, that's too bad, Joe, and I don't know of a thing we can do about it. Bring the bill down to the office, though, and it may help catch the man who's passing them. By the way, how's the tourist business out there?"

"Fine, Sheriff. Just fine!"

"Glad to hear it, Joe. Well, you bring that bill around and we'll see what we can do."

I hung up, amazed at how easy a lie could roll once you got it started. I did have a counterfeit five-dollar bill, of course. I'd been carrying it in my billfold almost a year, wondering what I was going to do with it.

Well, now I knew. That bogus bill, the way I figured it, was going to be worth about ten thousand dollars! It had got me off the hook with the sheriff. Because of that bill, and some pretty fast thinking, I'd soon be able to kick this town in the face. I'd soon be on my way to the top!

I felt like a million dollars, just thinking about it.

It seemed fantastic that the idea hadn't come to me right away, as soon as I'd heard Sheldon and Manley scheming the robbery. But it hadn't it had come at the very last minute, and it had been a damn near thing, too. This was the break I'd been waiting for, that beautiful once-in-a-lifetime break, and I had almost muffed it!

The trouble was I hadn't expected a break to come in the

form of a payroll robbery. What I had been expecting was the Herb Carter story all over again, but I knew now that breaks don't come spelled out for you—sometimes you've got to fill out the instructions yourself. Another thing; I hadn't expected my big break to land me on the wrong side of the law. But what the hell! Hadn't Herb Carter broken just about every law in the book? And had anything happened to him? Like hell it had. They're not so anxious to wave that law in your face if they know you've got a bankroll to fight with.

Anyway, I'd finally got it straight in my mind, and I felt fine about it. I walked around grinning. Oh, Sheldon and Manley were going to squeal like pigs under a fence when I broke the news to them that I was cutting myself in for one third of that box-factory payroll. But there was very little they could do about it. They'd either have to accept my terms or give up the jot)—and I just couldn't see a professional giving up a soft touch like that box factory.

I walked around in a rosy daze the rest of the afternoon. Good-by, filling station, good-by, tourist shacks, good-by, Creston! In another week I'd shake the whole business out of my hair.

But, in the meantime, I had to sit tight. I had to wait for the Sheldons to come back, and I had to act completely normal. That's the important thing, just act as though nothing at all had happened.

So I spent the rest of the day trying to act normal, trying to keep my feet on the ground. I stood in the station doorway, drank Cokes, watched the traffic go by. I thought about that robbery, and the ten thousand dollars, and getting away from Creston. And I also did a good deal of thinking about Paula Sheldon.

But I concentrated on acting normal. Every few minutes somebody from Creston would go by on the highway, and I'd wave, and then I'd think: Christ, what would they do if they knew what I'm thinking right now! They wouldn't believe it. What if I walked up to them and said, "Look here, on the fourteenth of this month I'm going to take part in a robbery. I'm going to help rob old Provo's payroll. What do you think of that?"

I wanted to laugh. They wouldn't believe it! Doc Hooper's boy robbing a payroll? Never!

If they only knew! I thought.

I made a kind of game out of it and amused myself for a while, but after a few hours it began to grow a little thin. Anyway, my thoughts always turned back to Paula Sheldon.

I kept remembering what she had said about her husband. "I don't love him at all," she had said. And she had meant it. And she had meant it when she had pressed that red mouth of hers to mine—there was no faking an excitement like that!

I knew what she was, and it made no difference at all. She was hard, as ruthless as she was beautiful, as brittle as fine china. Well, I could be hard too, and ruthless, and brittle. I had taken it on the chin plenty trying to play according to the rules. Now, for the first time in my life, I felt strong; I felt that I could do something really big, and to hell with the rulebooks.

But it all came back to Paula, eventually. Oh, I had been drunk on heady wine, all right, and only a man with a hangover can know the terrible thirst for more that comes the day after. Paula had known. Knowing that I never intended to keep my promise to her, she had smiled.

She had known better.

It's possible to hate and love at the same time, they say, but I did not hate Paula. Where there had been stale existence, Paula had brought excitement. She had given me something to fight for—herself. Let's face it, Hooper, it's not only the ten thousand dollars that fascinates you— it's that blonde as well, and you know it.

Her husband? I hardly thought of him. What was necessary I would do. But after the robbery Paula would belong to me.


Ike Abrams rattled off the highway in his '46 Ford, drove around to the back of the station, and parked beside the grease rack. I went around to meet him. "Can you take over now, Ike? I've got some things to do. We can check the cash register after a while."

"Sure," he said. "You sick or somethin', Joe? You look a little green around the rills."

"I feel fine."

I went to my cabin and didn't even notice the heat. I lay across the bed for several minutes without moving, without batting an eye, just staring at the ceiling and thinking of all the things I could do with one third of thirty thousand dollars. Ten thousand dollars, right in my pocket! It was more money than I'd ever had, more money than I'd ever seen, even, all at one time.

I must have dozed for a while. It was almost sundown when a knock at the door brought me out of it. I sat up, groggy with sleep and half dazed by the heat, and then I saw my father standing on the steps on the other side of the screen door.

"Son, you in there?"

"Sure, Dad. Come on in, if you can stand the heat."

I was still sitting there scratching my head as he opened the screen and stepped inside. "By God," I said, "I must have been crazy to go to sleep in this heat. I feel like I'd been knocked down with a wooden mallet. Sit down, Dad. I think there's some beer in the icebox."

He looked older than the last time I had seen him, which had been only a day or two before, and very tired. He smiled faintly, dropped into a cane-bottomed chair, and carefully placed his black satchel on the floor.

"Yes. I think* a beer might taste good."

I went to the kitchen and washed my face at the sink, then got the beers out of the icebox and brought them in. I dropped on the bed again and for one quiet moment we drank from the sweating cans. I was used to having my father drop in on me like this, every time he had a call out this way. He was the finest man I ever knew— and the only man in the world that I cared a damn about. We never said much. Usually it was just like this, sitting, drinking a beer together, and then he'd leave. I had a feeling, though, that today was going to be different.

"You been out to the Jarvis farm again?" I asked firmly.

He shrugged and smiled that small smile. "The McClellans, this time. The youngest boy stepped on a nail. Luckily, he had been vaccinated for tetanus."

"Why," I asked, "do you keep fooling with these hard-scrabble farmers, Dad? You'll never get your pay, and you know it. You could have a fine practice in town, be making plenty of money, if you'd stay in your office where people could find you."

He glanced at me, then away. "People in the country need doctors too. Besides, it's a little late for me to start making money, isn't it?"

"You could think about your health. It's not too late for that, but it will be pretty soon, if you keep making these farm calls at all hours."

We'd been over it a thousand times and had never found a meeting place. Maybe I would have been a doctor, the way he had wanted, if I could have seen any future in it when I was younger. But getting up at all hours of the night, when you're dead tired, and going out to the very end of God's nowhere to help some farmer's wife have her tenth kid was not my idea of a way to live.

"Joe ..." I looked up, almost forgetting that he was still sitting there. He cleared his throat and looked down at his lean, white hands. "Joe, I had a talk with Beth's father yesterday."

"Steve Langford?" I knew what he was thinking. I didn't want to talk about it. It was the last thing I wanted to discuss right now, with Paula Sheldon whirling in my mind, but I couldn't think of any way to stop it. "What did Langford have to talk about—that front yard of his?" I laughed. "You'd think it was his life's work, the time he puts on it."

"No." He still looked at his hands. "He talked about you, Joe, and about Beth."

"I know," I said, trying hard to keep a hold on my anger. "Langford wants to know if Beth and I have set the date yet. Well, I've got news for Langford. There's not going to be any date. What a hell of a town this is! Go out with a girl a few times and they've got you as good as married!"

I had plenty more to say. I was getting damn tired of people like Steve Langford butting in on my business. But I left them unsaid, the things that were in my mind. I had no wish to hurt my father, the one man in the world that I liked. I guess he figured, like Langford, that someday I would marry a home-town girl and settle down to rot the rest of my life away in Creston. Well, he was mistaken about that; they all were mistaken.

But the look of disappointment in my father's eyes shook me. I suddenly realized how old he was, and tired, and finally I said: "I'll tell you what I'll do. I'll talk it over with Beth."

He smiled, very faintly. "All right, Joe. Whatever you say." Then he reached for his satchel and stood up. We said the usual small things, and after a while he was gone.

I was late, as usual, when I got around to the Langford place that night, and as usual Steve Langford was watering his front lawn as I drove up.

"You're late tonight, Joe."

"Got held up at the station again," I said.

He seemed distant, cool. He had been doing a lot of thinking and had just about decided that he didn't like me.

"Beth's in the house, I think." He went on with his watering.

I sat in the car waiting for Beth to come out. Something made me look at Langford again. He was standing half crouched, rigid as a statue, with the squirting nozzle in his hands, almost as though it were a gun. I got it then. He was waiting for me to get out of the car, walk up to the front porch, and meet his daughter at the door.

Well, I thought, the hell with him! I tramped the horn button and the blaring sound hit the silent dusk like a hammer. Bright crimson rushed to Langford's face as he stood there. I tramped the horn again, just for the hell of it. By God, I thought, if she doesn't want to come out of the house, that's fine with me!

But she came out. I knew she was defying her father in doing it, but she came out.

"Are you ready?" I said.

"Sure, Joe." Not looking at her father, she walked head down to the Chevy and got into the front seat beside me.

That was all we said until we were away from the house. She sat stiff and silent as I worked the Chevy toward the highway. She looked clean and crisp in a white dress, and her tanned arms and small face made her look almost like a young girl. But she certainly was no Paula Sheldon.

Well, I thought, I'm glad the end is in sight. And Beth knew it—it was written in the strained lines of her face. She was thirty years old, which is pretty old for a single girl in a town like Creston, and I could see it written in those lines of desperation at the corners of her mouth, in the steady glassiness of her eyes. There was just one thing I wished for: I wanted it to be calm and civilized. I had no wish to hurt her—all I wanted was to end it as cleanly as possible.

About three miles out of town we turned off the highway, onto a graveled road, and before long we could see the dark stand of oak and blackjack that more or less surrounded Lake

Creston. It was getting dark now and we began meeting cars heading back toward town, some of them towing small boats on two-wheeled trailers. Local fishermen.

Pretty soon we could see the lake itself, a pretty good-sized body of water for that part of the country, sprawling over maybe three hundred acres and held in check by a big dirt dam. I glanced at Beth, and she looked surprised. It had been a long time since I had brought her out here.

Maybe it was a mistake to come to this particular place, but it was the only place I could think of where we could talk and not be disturbed—where we could get mad and yell at each other, if it came to that, and not be afraid that somebody would hear us. I made a great business of watching the road as the lake rose up before us.

It was always something of a shock to see that much water in a dry country. The lake had been built back in the thirties by the WPA. It furnished Creston with water, and was well stocked for fishing, and a few years back picnic grounds had been constructed below the dam. There was a dock where several fishing boats, and even a few snipe-class sailboats, were tied up. Up toward the head of the dam there was a small blockhouse where you could buy fish bait, fishing licenses, and beer. I stopped and picked up a can of beer before crossing the dam. Now that the sun had set, the night was almost cool near the water.

"You want to take a turn around the lake?" I said.

She said something, I didn't hear what, as I circled the car to get under the wheel. "It's really quite a place," I said. "I wouldn't mind having a cabin out here somewhere, a place where a guy could knock off for a day or so and just take it easy."

I was just killing time, and Beth knew it. I could feel her staring at me, wondering what I was going to say.

There was a narrow, single-lane graveled road that meandered all the way around the lake, and now and then a deep-rutted spur that wandered off to a dead end at some abandoned farm. I put the car in gear and started across the dam, dunking vaguely that the cabin idea wasn't a bad one, at that. Maybe Paula and I would get ourselves one sometime. It would take some money, of course, but Old Man Provo and his box factory were going to furnish that.

After we hit the lake road we had to take it easy. It was dark, and the road crawled crazily in and out of wild-looking blackjack thickets, and you had to watch for cars parked here and there along the road. High-school kids.

About halfway around the lake I pulled my Chevy onto one of those abandoned farm roads and snapped out the lights. I looked at Beth, then lit a cigarette and sat back in the seat. There was tightness around her mouth, a determined look in her eyes.

"Joe."

I looked at her.

"Joe, what's wrong? Something is wrong, isn't there? You've hardly said a word since we left the house."

I didn't know how to say it. Goddamnit, I thought, I should have just called her on the telephone and told her it was all over. She moved over next to me, and I was the stiff one now, and cold.

"Joe..."

"Yes?"

"What is it, Joe? Can't you tell me?"

The situation was ridiculous, and being ridiculous made me mad. "Christ," I said, "do I have to spell it out for you? We're not getting anywhere, that's all, and your old man thinks we ought to knock it off." I looked straight ahead, through the windshield. "I think so, too."

She did nothing for several seconds, sitting very erect, clenching her hands in her lap. Then, finally: "Joe, is it someone else? I know what my father thinks, and it isn't important, but is it someone else?"

"Now, who else would it be?" I said wearily. "If I'd found someone else, it would be all over Creston by now and you know it."

"But... there must be a reason!"

"I told you," I said. "We're not getting anywhere. And I'm tired of not getting anywhere, tired of Creston, tired of those lousy tourist shacks. I'm leaving this country, Beth, and everything in it. It's as simple as that."

"Is it, Joe?"

"Now, what's that supposed to mean? Of course it's as

simple as that. I'm sick of it and I'm leaving it."

"And me, Joe?" A very tight voice. "What about me?"

Good Lord, I thought, what do you have to say to a woman like this?

I said, "It's over. If there was ever anything to begin with. That's what I'm trying to tell you. It's over."

She didn't believe me. Womanlike, she couldn't believe that after all this time she was being dumped. Behind it all, she probably believed that my motivations were noble and gallant, because she couldn't make herself believe that I was simply sick of her and that was the whole story.

Then she did a hell of a thing. You had to know Beth to understand what a hell of a thing it was. Suddenly she had her arms around my neck and was pressing herself against me, and there was absolutely no mistake about what she had in her mind. This was her one big weapon—the one weapon that all nice girls like Beth hold onto to the bitter end, hoping that they'll never have to use it but firmly convinced that it will gain them their ends, a ring and marriage certificate, if the time should ever come.

It left me completely cold. Instantly, Paula was in my brain again, and nothing in the world that Beth could do could stir me. I reached for the switch and snapped it on.

"You might as well go on saving it," I said. "But for somebody else."

# Chapter Four

The fourteenth was a long time coming that July. The days dragged as I stood in the station doorway watching the traffic go past, thinking: Maybe the next car will be that Buick, maybe the Sheldons will come early to make sure there are no slip-ups.

Then I'd get to thinking: Maybe they won't come back at all. Maybe something happened and they decided to call the whole thing off.

What would I do then? They *had* to come! I couldn't stand this lousy place much longer. I couldn't stand this flea-bitten service station. I wanted to feel that money in my pocket. I wanted Paula close to me, where I could reach out and touch her.

Meanwhile, I was alone. That business with Beth at the lake—Lord, I hope I never get into a mess like that again. She cried. She didn't say a single word, just lay there with great tears streaming down that pale, pinched face of hers. I had hated her at the time, but now I felt nothing. I hadn't heard a word from Bern since that night. I knew I never would.

Now there was the robbery to be thought about. I wasn't worried about Manley and Sheldon; I was holding all the cards. If they pulled the robbery, there was no way they could keep me out of it. And they would pull it, all right, because Paula would have it no other way.

Still, I was taking no chances.

On the thirteenth I decided to do something that I should have done at the very beginning. I was going over that box factory with a fine-tooth comb. I wasn't going to rely on Bunt Manley.

I thought: This is going to look damn funny, Hooper. You haven't been near that factory since you stopped working there. Is this going to be smart, sticking your nose into things the day before the robbery?

Smart or not, I couldn't take chances on something going wrong. And about that time I remembered Pat Sully—good old Pat Sully, who had loaned me five dollars six months ago and had probably kissed it good-by long since.

Well, Pat was going to get a surprise, because I was going to pay him back, and I was going to pay him back because he happened to be a bookkeeper for Max Provo and did his work in the factory's front office, which was exactly the place I wanted to visit.About three that afternoon I turned the station over to Ike Abrams and took the Chevy into town. The factory was north and west of town, sprawled out on the red slope of a clay bill. There were two main buildings, two-story red-brick affairs, connected by a plank runway at the second-story level.

One building was the factory itself, where the boxes were made, and that one didn't interest me at all. The other was a conglomeration of warehouse-garage-storeroom-office, and this one interested me plenty.

I parked the Chevy in the company parking space at the west side of the factory, got out, and started walking around to where the front office was. There was a good deal of activity at the loading ramp, where two big semis were backed up to be loaded. Sweating roustabouts formed an endless chain with their loaded dollies, warehouse to trailer and back again, working like so many ants around an anthill. I had been one of those ants once. Never again. The office itself was a busy place and not much to look at. It was just one big room, the working space partitioned off by wooden railings. Truck drivers and warehousemen were coming and going, and some of them were trying to make themselves heard over the noise of typewriters- and adding machines. There were maybe a dozen girls on one side of the room, filing things, typing letters, or whatever they do in an office like that; and on the other side of the room the bookkeepers and department managers were going about their business and ignoring everything else.

The temperature must have been a hundred in that room. No air-conditioning, not even an electric fan. Those things cost money, and anything that cost money wasn't for Max Provo.

I had been in that office a hundred times or more, but this time I really looked at it. There was a big double door at the back of the office; one of the doors was open— for better ventilation—and I could look into the warehouse, on the other side of the plyboard partition. Nothing had changed since I had worked here. Everything was the same, but this time I was taking a picture of it in my mind.

"Then my gaze landed on the thing I was really looking for, the safe.

It looked like a hell of a safe to me. It looked like the great-great-grandfather of all the safes in the world. I had seen it before, I must have seen it before, but I didn't remember it as being that big. It was the biggest, heaviest, ruggedest-looking damn safe I'd ever seen. It was six feet tall; at least six feet tall, and almost as wide, and there was no telling how thick or heavy the thing was. It looked as big as a Sherman tank.

That Sheldon better be good, I thought, because it's going to take more than a can opener to get into that thing.

"Hello, Joe. Not lookin' for a job, are you?"

I looked, around and there was a man grinning at me from me other side of the railing, a little sharp-faced, stoop-shouldered man whose name was Paul Killman and who, so the story went, rode in on the first load of brick when they started building the box factory thirty years ago and had been there ever since.

I said, "Hello, Mr. Killman. I.just happened to be passing this way and remembered that I wanted to see Pat Sully about something. Do you know where he is?"

"Why, I think he's at his desk. Yes, there he is."

I'd been so busy looking at that safe that I hadn't seen Pat at all. But I saw him now, a big, red-faced guy about my own age, sleepily putting figures inter an open ledger.

"All right if I talk to him a minute?" I asked.

"Sure, sure, Joe. You know your way around here."

I pushed open the gate and went around on the business side of the railing. I put a five-dollar bill on Pat's ledger and said, "The age of miracles hasn't passed, after all, and here's something to prove it. Remember that five you loaned me?"

His head snapped up. "Hell, Joe, you didn't have to come all the way out here to give it to me. To tell the truth, I'd forgotten all about it."

Like hell he had. He was quick enough to put it in his pocket.

We talked for maybe five minutes about things that neither of us cared a damn about. Pat kept looking anxiously at Old Man Provo's desk, in the far corner of the room, as though he expected the sky to fall. I was sizing up that room. I was getting a picture of it in my mind that couldn't be erased. That safe was the only thing that bothered me.

I said, "Is the water cooler still in the warehouse? Let's go back and have a cigarette. Old Provo can get along without you for a few minutes."

Pat didn't like it much; old Provo was hell on getting his pound of flesh from the office force. Then he shrugged. Maybe he was getting tired of the job anyway. "All right, but just for a minute."

I wanted to get a good look at that warehouse, because that was the way we had to come in. We couldn't come in the front way; that was well lighted and facing the highway. It had to be the back way, through the warehouse. I deliberately counted the steps from Pat's desk, which was about in the center of the room, to the warehouse partition.

I swung close enough to the safe to get the brand name; it was a Kimble. A Kimble Monarch, the lettering said, Model K-467. It was an elephant of a safe. Why hadn't I noticed it before? No wonder the place had never been robbed, with a safe like that. If you're smart, I thought, you'll drop this thing right where it is. Let Manley and Sheldon beat their brains out trying to get inside that iron blockhouse. It's crazy to think that a man could ever open a monster like that.

Then I was crazy, because I was not dropping it now. Sheldon was the expert on safes; let *him* worry about it.

The water cooler was a big galvanized can with two spigots at the bottom, sitting on a couple of sawhorses just on the other side of the office partition, in the warehouse itself. Entering that warehouse was like stepping into the bleak, empty spaces of a desert. It looked as big as those hangars they used to house dirigibles in. The ceiling was two stories high, and up there somewhere, in the gloom, cranes rolled back and forth, the noise echoing and bouncing from one wall to the other. All over the floor there were skeleton crates filled with flattened cardboard cartons of every size and shape imaginable, and the roustabouts were continually bringing them in or taking them out.

At the back of the building there was a giant steel sliding door, and I immediately counted that out. A door like that might turn out to be tougher to open than the safe. That left the windows, and they didn't look much better. To start with, they were small, and they had iron bars on them.

I stood there at the water cooler talking to Pat, but I don't know what about. I was studying those windows at the back of the warehouse. Then one of the workers, a big swarthy guy in overalls, saw me and yelled.

He had a grin a yard wide. His name was Matt Souel and he had been just another roustabout when I had worked at the factory, but now he was the warehouse foreman.

"What the hell you doin' out here with us workin' folks, Joe?"

Pat Sully was nervous and happy enough to make a quick excuse and get back on the job before Provo discovered that he was missing. I went back and talked to Matt Souel for a while, glad that he had called to me. It gave me a chance to have a closer look at those rear windows.

We'd wake the whole town trying to get past those iron bars. But the thing that really decided me had nothing to do with the bars. The thing that decided me was about twenty feet of makeshift electrical wiring and an oblong box fixed to the rear wall, above the windows.

There were limits, it seemed, to how far even a man like Max Provo would go to save money. He was tight, all right, but he hadn't been too tight to invest in a burglar alarm.

The windows were out.

Everything was out unless I could find a way of disconnecting, that burglar alarm, and I didn't know a damn thing about burglar alarms. I didn't know where the switch was, or how it was set, or anything else. And even if I did know, I couldn't very well start fooling with that wiring when there were fifteen or twenty roustabouts looking on.

Matt Souel was still talking, and I stood there grinning like an idiot while my spirits sank like a truck falling down an elevator shaft.

Hell, I thought, we're beat even before we start. If the back of this building is wired, then so is the front. Touch one of those doors or windows after closing time and the whole town is going to know about it. You'll have Otis Miller and the rest of the police force on your back before you know what hit you.

Then I remembered something. I remembered the garage,

on the other side of the warehouse, and I remembered the two master switch boxes that controlled the electrical output to both buildings. They were in the garage. And the garage wasn't locked at night, because that was where the night watchman stayed most of the time.

I was beginning to feel better. I felt fine. Burglar alarms were electrically operated; all we had to do was open the circuit to this warehouse building, and you could knock the walls down and the burglar alarms wouldn't do a thing.

I felt great. I felt like a man whose parachute had finally opened a hundred feet above the ground. Not even those barred windows worried me now. Not even that steel monster of a safe could worry me.

The next day, about four in the afternoon, the blue Buick pulled under the station shed and Karl Sheldon said pleasantly, "Here we are again. I hope you've got a vacancy for us."

I felt as big as a house. I grinned right in his face and said, "Yes, sir, I've been saving one for you."

Paula was back in shorts again, white duck shorts and white T shirt and thong sandles. Just looking at her was all I needed to get me excited again. She didn't say a word. She just sat there smiling that slow smile, knowing that she was being stared at and liking it.

She knew what I was thinking, all right. She knew what was in my mind.

Sheldon said, "We're in luck, honey. He's saved a place for us."

You sonofabitch, I thought. Do you think I'm so stupid that I don't know sarcasm when I hear it? I was tempted to hit him with it right there. I wanted to grab him by the throat and say, "Listen to me, you pompous bastard, I'm cutting myself in for one third of your take tonight. What do you think of that?"

But I played it straight. I signed them in, then took them to the cabin.

Sheldon came around to the back of the car and began unlocking the trunk. I didn't offer to help. Somewhere in that car there was enough nitroglycerin to blow us to hell, and I wanted no part of it. I unlocked the cabin and opened some windows.

When I turned around, Paula was standing right behind me. I grabbed her.

I hadn't meant to. I had it all planned not to do a thing until I got everything settled with Sheldon. But I simply couldn't keep my hands off her. That bright hot arc jumped between us and suddenly she was straining against me.

"You haven't changed," she said huskily.

"It's been a long time."

"Only a week."

"Do you know how long a week can be?"

"Yes, I know.""

That ripe mouth didn't slip away this time as I kissed her. I felt her nails digging into my shoulders again, into my arms. "You're strong, aren't you, Joe? Hard and strong."

"Yes."

"I believe it. I've thought about you, Joe. Your arms like leather rope. I like men with arms like that."

"You've got some points too that I've thought about."

Her arms went around my neck and pulled tight. The words came through her teeth. "There's no future in this, Joe. You know that, don't you?"

"We'll talk about that later."

"There won't be any later. Tomorrow I'll be gone. Besides, there's Karl."

"You said you didn't love him."

"That has nothing to do with it."

I had the feeling that she didn't like what was happening, but she was unable to stop it, just as I was unable to stop it. A handful of iron gets caught in an electrical field and jumps to the magnet. The iron has nothing to say about it.

Outside, an impatient horn blared out, and I knew it was somebody at the station wanting gas or oil. Then Sheldon called, "Hooper, you've got a customer."

I had forgotten about Sheldon, the station, and everything else. Sheldon hit the steps, but before he got the door open Paula was out of my arms. She threw herself on the bed and lay there like a marble statue, as white and unmoving as marble statue, that red mouth of hers partly open.

She lay there on her back, her arms and legs forming a white letter X on the bed, her eyes closed. For just a moment I remembered some paintings that I had seen once. They were nudes, painted by some Italian with a name I couldn't pronounce. The nude women all looked alike and they were all painted orange; their bodies, their faces, every thing was orange but the hair, and they were the nakedest women I ever saw.

Sheldon was in the room now, standing there by the door. I looked at him but couldn't tell what he was thinking.

"I think you've got a customer," he said again.

"Yes. I heard."

I'd have to wait until Ike relieved me at the station before I could hit him with the robbery business. Anyway, I needed to calm down a little. I got out of there.

I went back to the station, took care of the customer, and tried to keep my feet on the ground until Ike came. I didn't hear any noise from the Number 2 cabin, so I figured Sheldon hadn't noticed anything out of the way. I didn't give a damn whether he had or not.

Maybe fifteen minutes had passed when Sheldon backed the Buick out of the carport and headed toward town. That meant he was going to make his contact with Manley and get their plans jelled.

Sheldon had been gone almost an hour when the telephone rang.

"Hooper?"

"Yes." I didn't recognize the voice at first.

"This is Karl Sheldon. Would you give my wife a message for me?"

"Sure, Mr. Sheldon."

"Just tell her that some important business has come up and our plans have been changed. Please ask her to get everything packed and I'll be back as soon as possible."

"You're checking out, Mr. Sheldon?"

"That's right. Sorry if we've inconvenienced you, Hooper, but of course we'll pay the usual rental fee."

"I see."

I didn't see worth a damn. But something had gone wrong. Something had exploded right in my face and I didn't know what it was. All I could think of was that I had to talk to Paula and talk fast before her husband of back. Maybe, between the two of us, we could straighten the thing out.

Then Ike Abrams drove up in that jalopy of his, and I was never so glad to see anybody in my life. I turned the station over to Ike, then went to my own cabin, as I always did. When I saw that Ike was busy in front of the station I went over to the Sheldon's cabin.

Paula was still on the bed, but she came off it the minute I stepped through the door.

"Something's wrong," I said. "Your husband just called and said for you to get packed."

"What?"

"That's all he said. He's checking out as soon as he gets back and he wants you to get packed. Do you know what it means?"

Something happened to that beautiful face of hers; it wasn't so beautiful now. "Yes," she said, almost hissed. "I know what it means. It means he's backed out on the factory job."

"Why would he do a thing like that?"

"Because everything has to be perfect. If everything isn't absolutely perfect, he won't touch it."

"I still don't get it," I said.

I had never seen anger just like hers. It was almost as though she could turn it off and on by throwing a switch. Now she switched it off, sat on the edge of the bed, and put her hand to her forehead. "I really can't blame him so much. He spent five years in a cell for making a mistake once, and he doesn't want to make any more. Probably Bunt Manley couldn't get the information he wanted, so he called it off."

"Just like that he'd turn thumbs down on thirty thousand dollars?"

"It's more than thirty thousand dollars—it's his life."

I remembered what Paula had said about how much it had cost to get her husband a parole. "It's the string-pullers you're worried about, isn't it? What happens to your husband if they don't get paid?"

"They always get paid, one way or another."

"How much time does he have?"

She looked up. "It ran out a week ago. Karl thinks he can outrun them, but I know better."

It would suit me fine to let the string-pullers take cafe of Sheldon in their own way, but I needed him myself. That safe had to have an expert's attention, and Sheldon was the only expert I knew.

"This is important to you, isn't it?" I said.

I am convinced that she could read my mind. "No, Joe. Not you!"

"What's the matter with me? Am I made of old china? Do I go to pieces when I'm dropped? You say you're not in love with your husband—that's good enough for me. Maybe you'll tell me someday why you're so concerned about him, but that isn't important now. If I get your husband off the hook by convincing him that this job can be brought off, with my help, would you drop him?" "For you, Joe?" "For me."

For one long moment she said nothing. Then, without looking at me, she said, "You wouldn't like it, Joe. I would want things that you couldn't give me."

"Don't believe it. All I need is a little time." "You wouldn't like my world," she said. "You wouldn't like me, either, after you got to know me."

"The way I feel about you has nothing to do with liking you. I just have to have you. As for this world of yours, all I ask is that it be different from the one I've known all my life."

I moved in front of her, lifted her chin, and made her look at me. "You've been in my brain ever since I first saw you. After that night in my cabin I started cutting myself away from Creston and everything connected with it."

She smiled faintly. "You're a convincing man, Joe." "It's a deal?"

She nodded. "It's a deal, as you say. Now tell me how you're going to convince Karl."

That was when we heard the Buick outside. It pulled into the carport beside the cabin and I said, "I won't have to tell you. You can see for yourself."

Sheldon was surprised to find me there with his wife, but not too much surprised. He said, "Well, Hooper..." then stepped over to the table and put down a brief case and some papers. Maybe he was used to walking into situations like this. He eased into a chair at the table and Paula lay across the bed, her eyes alive, her body, tense.

Sheldon said, "Did you want to see me about something, Hooper?"

"Yes."

"Well, out with it."

The way he said it did something to me. A spring snapped. The words came out like pistol shots. "All right Sheldon, here it is. It has to do with you and me and an ex-convict named Bunt Manley. It has to do with a box factory and a thirty-thousand-dollar payroll. Does any of that ring a bell?"

He was surprised this time and showed it.

"I'm afraid I don't know what you're talking about."

I was impatient now and wanted to get it over with. "Look," I said, coming toward him. "I know what you and Manley are planning to do. It would scare hell out of you to know how close I came to telling the police. But I didn't. I got to thinking."

I let it hang, watching Sheldon's face. One second it was red with rage, and then it was gray. Paula sat up on the bed, her mouth half open, looking as though she were going to laugh.

She didn't laugh. After a moment she lay back on her elbows and stared at me, not making a move, not even blinking.

Sheldon's anger was pretty thin when he said, "I think you're crazy, Hooper. I still don't know what you're talking about."

"Goddamnit! I haven't thought this thing out just for the sake of argument. Get that through your head, will you? I came here to talk business."

He'd had a pretty bad shock, but he was quick to regain his poise. He began putting things together, slowly at first, and then it came with a rush, like a summer storm, and he had the whole picture.

He looked at me and a suggestion of a sneer began to form at the corners of his mouth.

"You punks," he said hoarsely. "You all think you can ride luck, nothing but luck, to the very top, but you never think of the long fall down. Eavesdropping must be very interesting, Hooper. You must hear some interesting things in these cabins, even some profitable things, maybe, although I doubt that you have the brains or imagination to bring them off."

I almost hit him. He was big and in good condition, but I could have taken him. But I didn't. I snapped a steel trap on my temper and held it.

I said, "I think we should talk business."

"With a punk like you, Hooper?" He looked as though he might laugh, but didn't. Instead, he dropped back into his chair and sat there looking at me, shaking his head.

I said, "There's thirty thousand dollars in that factory, Sheldon. That's ten thousand a man, not bad for about an hour's work."

I could see that he wasn't going for it. He wasn't the kind to let himself be pushed into a thing he didn't like. My ground was falling out from under me.

Then I noticed the papers that Sheldon had put on the table, and I could see, what they were. There was a detailed diagram of the factory layout, streets and highway, and there were other sketches that I took to be diagrams of the office interior and warehouse. I took a step forward and scooped up a fistful of the papers. When I straightened up I was looking into the muzzle of a .38.

It was a Police Special. Most of the bluing had been worn off around the muzzle and the front sight had been filed off even with the barrel. In Sheldon's brown hand it looked businesslike and deadly.

"Those papers," he said, holding out his free hand.

"You've already talked to Manley, haven't you?" I said. "You didn't like the way he laid it out, so you called off the job."

I studied that pistol for one long second, then handed him the papers.

"You punks," he said again. "I don't know anyone named Manley. I don't know anything about a box factory. I'm just a tourist who made the mistake of spending the night in this rat trap of yours—and after these papers are burned, you can't prove I'm anything else. Besides, I don't think you'll holler cop, Hooper. You'd have a bit of explaining to do yourself."

He smiled.

The robbery *couldn't* be called off! My whole future was built on this one thing, this one night. Without its support, all my tomorrows would come crashing down.

"Look." I hardly recognized the voice as my own. Sheldon still had that pistol in his hand, but I ignored it now. "Look," I said again, and stepped right in front of him, right in front of the muzzle of that gun, "look at these sketches." I grabbed them from his hand, scattered them out on the table. Then, with one sweep, I brushed them all on the floor. "I told you I was here to talk business," I said. Get me some paper and a pencil, and I'll prove it."

For one long moment he did nothing. I could see a thousand things going on behind his eyes, like lemons and plums and bells whirling past the windows of a slot machine. Paula still lay back on her elbows, staring with a kind of dumb fascination.

Then, at last, things stopped happening behind Sheldon's eyes. I heard the soft sound of breath whistling between his teeth. There was a little click as he switched the safety on that .38, then he slipped the pistol into his waistband and said, "Get it for him, Paula. Pencil and paper."

Paula got up lazily, almost bored now that the moment of tenseness was over. She got several sheets of note paper and a fountain pen out of one of the suitcases and brought them over to the table. Sheldon didn't say a thing. He just waited. I picked up the pen and went to work.

I had the inside of that office and warehouse and garage down perfectly. I had stepped them off, I even had the approximate dimensions. I put it all on paper and shoved it over for Sheldon to look at.

Two full minutes must have passed before he said, "Are you sure about all this?"

"I was in the place yesterday. I made it my business to find out."

"And also to make a suspect of yourself." The sneer was beginning to show again.

"There's a guy in the place I know," I said. "I owed him five dollars and just dropped in to pay him."

The sneer disappeared. "What about the safe?"

"The biggest goddamn safe I ever saw. A Kimble Monarch, Model K-four-six-seven."

He began to relax. He even smiled, very faintly. "Given time, I could open it with a nail file. However, that won't be necessary. What about burglar alarms?"

"The place is wired, all right, front and back. But the master switch box is in the garage, where the watchman stays. It shouldn't be much of a job to find the right switch and cut off the power to the building."

I could see that he was interested, and I began to breathe normally again. "When we cut off the power," J said, "it will darken the building, of course, but I don't think it will be noticed because the front of the factory is lighted with floodlights."

"How do we get in—*if* I should lose my mind and decide to try it your way?"

"Through the front door. It's the only way." "With all those floodlights?" An eyebrow lifted, that was all.

"I told you it's the only way. The back door is a big power-operated steel affair and out of the question. It would take all night to saw through the bars on the rear windows. What we'll have to do is take the keys from the watchman, watch our chance, and go right in the front door."

He wasn't even listening. He was back to studying that sketch I had drawn. Paula was standing behind him, looking over his shoulder.

"It looks all right," she said. "Everything you want is there."

Sheldon said nothing. He was thinking. "It's a lot better than your pal Manley could do," Paula went on.

Sheldon ignored the gentle prod about Manley. "It could be a soft touch," he said thoughtfully, "if something hasn't been overlooked. That could be a big *if*. I should have scouted the place myself. It was a mistake to leave it up to Manley."

"Manley!" Paula spat the name. "You were a fool to listen to an ox like Manley in the first place. He's smalltime. He'll never be anything else."

"But he spotted the factory," Sheldon said, as though he felt somehow obligated to defend Manley.

Paula said one word, a word that is not often heard, even among men. There was nothing sleepy or passive about her now. There was an almost electrical energy about her. She walked across the room, snapped a cigarette out of a pack, and lit it.

"Leave Manley out of it," she said. "Forget him. He's contributed nothing so he gets nothing."

Until now I had been satisfied to remain quiet and let Paula get my argument across. But this business about leaving Manley out of it was no good.

She took one nervous drag on the cigarette and then ground it out on the floor, ignoring an ash tray less than twelve inches away.

"I know what you're going to say, Hooper," she said to me, as though she had never seen me before. "That is your name, isn't it? You're going to say that we can't leave him out. But we will. Manley's a fool, all right, but he's not fool enough to yell cop in a situation like this. When he reads about the burglary in the morning paper, he may not like it, but there'll be nothing he can do about it."

I shook my head, and Sheldon started to speak, but she stopped both of us. "Think of that five thousand dollars, that extra five thousand that will be yours, Hooper, if we leave Manley out of this. Anyway, what are you afraid of? Manley doesn't know that you've cut yourself in. There's no way he could hurt you."

Sheldon managed to break in this time. "I'm afraid there's one small detail you've overlooked," he said. "I haven't decided to take this job."

"*I* have decided," Paula said. "We have to have that money, Karl. It's not too late to set yourself right with those people, but we've got to have the money!"

She could be beautiful and decorative when she wanted, but she could also be other things. We stood there looking at each other over Sheldon's head. She's a hell of a woman, I thought, realizing vaguely that my argument about Manley was slipping away from me. One hell of a woman!

## Chapter Five

I went back to my cabin feeling nine feet tall. Fifteen thousand dollars! What a man could do with that much money! I looked at my watch and saw that it was already six o'clock. I'd been in the Sheldon cabin almost two hours and the thing was settled.

Everything was all right, it was fine. Paula had everything, brains as well as looks. What a hell of a team we would make!

And then I saw Ike Abrams peering through the screen door. "Where the hell have you been, Joe? Your dad was around a while ago and we couldn't find you anywhere."

"Where have I been? Nowhere."

Wait a minute, I thought. That won't do. "Oh," I said, "I was over in Number Two. The shower was leaking again and they wanted me to fix it."

Just in case he had seen me go over there.

He kept standing there, one foot on the step and his face almost against the screen. "What is it?" I said. "Is something wrong?" '

"No, I guess not. It's just your father. He looked worried."

"He's always worried about something. Probably he's pulling another of his hard-scrabble farmers through another siege of malaria."

"I think he's worried about you, Joe." He had something on his chest and he wasn't going to rest till he got it out. He said, "I know this is none of my business, Joe, but if you and Beth have had a fallin' out about something, well, it's never too late to make up, they say."

"Great God!" I exploded. "Ike, will you get back to the station and stop sticking your long nose into my business?"

He looked as though I had pulled a knife on him. Backing away from the steps, he mumbled, "All right, Joe.... I'm sorry."

I hadn't realized I was so on edge. I almost called Ike back to apologize to him, but I didn't. What difference did it make? I was cutting away from Creston anyway.

I prowled the cabin for maybe thirty minutes, but the place

wasn't big enough to hold me. I wanted to see Paula. I wanted to make plans for the future—a future with just me and her and no Karl Sheldon. But I couldn't talk to her now, and I couldn't very well just sit in the cabin until time for the robbery.

I looked through the window and Paula was sitting on the steps of Number 2 again, but this time her husband was standing in the doorway behind her. What the hell, I thought. I pulled on a clean shirt and went out.

"Hooper?" Sheldon said.

"Yes?"

"What do you usually do this time of day?"

"Do? Nothing in particular, I guess."

He opened the screen door and stepped outside. "It's important," he said soberly, "to keep to your regular routine, if you have one. Are you sure there isn't some kind of pattern? Don't you have a girl friend in town that you see pretty often?"

I looked straight at Paula and she smiled faintly. "No, I don't have a girl friend."

"Then why don't you drive into town and see a movie, if you're not going to stay at the station? The less we see of each other, the less chance there is for suspicion. Just be sure you're back by midnight."

Maybe he was right. I had to do something to kill time, and sitting alone in my cabin was no way to do it. Of course, there was always the chance that I might get a few minutes alone with Paula if I stuck around, but odds were long. Everything would go to hell if he caught us together.

"All right," I said. "Midnight." I headed toward the station to get the Chevy.


It was the longest movie I ever sat through. It was the first time I had missed Beth, or even thought much about her, since I had made up my mind to break away. I was so used to having her sitting there beside me that it was almost like being lost. It was strange at first—but I had a cure for that.

All I had to do was think of Paula.

I didn't see a thing that happened on the screen; I just sat there and thought of what Paula and I would do after the robbery. Then I began thinking about the robbery itself, and that was when the first stirrings of uncertainty made themselves felt in my bowels. What if I had overlooked something at the factory! What if that switch had nothing to do with the burglar alarm at all? After all, I didn't know a damn thing about burglar alarms. Maybe the wiring on it was independent of the original circuits. What a hell of a thing that would be!

I never hated a thing in my life as much as I hated that movie. Every instinct told me to get out of there. Get out in the cool clean air and get this thing straightened out before it strangled.

That's just what I did, and it worked. The minute I got outside, the uncertainty was gone and I felt fine. I killed some time at a beer drive-in, then took a ride out north of town, and the first thing I knew there was the box factory looming up in the darkness. I don't know what had pulled me in that direction, but there I was.

Looking at it made my guts draw in a little. At night the place looked much more formidable than it did in the daytime, those two solid brick buildings squatting on a clay hillside. They looked almost prisonlike, with those floodlights pouring down the front of the main building, and I thought: I hope to hell that's not an omen.

I kept driving until I came to a section line and turned around. On the way back to town I tried not to look at it, but the thing was too big, too formidable to ignore. How were we ever going to get inside the place with all those floodlights pointed right at the front door? I had seen the factory a hundred times at night, but I had never noticed that there were so many of those floodlights or that they were so bright.

Then I thought of all that money. Thirty thousand dollars, maybe more. I thought of what Paula and I could do with money like that, and it would be just a beginning. The factory didn't look so tough after that. I drove straight through town and headed for the station. It was getting close to midnight.

## Chapter Six

Karl Sheldon said: "Have you got a gun?"

"We don't need guns to take care of the watchman."

"I hope you're right. But in case you're not, take this."

It was a nicely blued Colt's .38, and it looked as though it had never been fired. "I'll take it," I said. "But I'm telling you now, I'm not going to use it."

He looked at me. "Let's hope not." It was almost a prayer, the way he said it.

The time was twelve minutes past midnight and the three of us were back in Number 2 cabin. Paula still had on those white shorts and halter and was lounging on the bed.

"Well," Sheldon said, "I guess there's no use waiting."

"I guess not."

He took up a satchel, similar to the one my father carried his medical supplies in, and the two of us went out the door. Paula said nothing. She lay there on one elbow, her eyes quick and alive, but she didn't make a sound.

"We'll take the Buick," Sheldon said. "You drive."

I got under the wheel and Sheldon sat on the other side, holding the satchel very carefully in his lap. "There's one thing," I said, before pressing the starter. "This old night watchman, he's kind of a friend of mine. He might recognize me, so you'll have to take care of him. Tie him up or something, but don't hurt him."

"My friend," Sheldon said dryly, "I understand that they have not yet installed a lethal gas chamber in your state penitentiary, and the electric chair is a very nasty way to die. You may be assured that I want no part of murder."

"I'm glad we understand each other." I started the car.

The traffic on Highway 66 was very thin, and there was almost none at all in Creston, but I played it safe anyway. I didn't want to be seen driving that Buick, so I took the side streets through town until we hit the north highway. Sheldon seemed lost in thought and neither of us said anything until we saw those floodlights in front of the box factory.

Then he said, "Keep in the shadows as much as possible and drive around to the back, where we can't be seen from the highway."

"Do you think I'm crazy enough to park under those floodlights?"

He looked at me coldly. I was just about ready to turn onto the factory road when a car topped the hill ahead of us, headed toward Creston. I had to drive on to the next section line, turn around, and try again. This time there were no cars. I tried not to look at those floodlights as I shoved the Buick into second and skidded onto the graveled factory road.

"Take it easy, you fool!" Sheldon snapped. "There's enough nitro in this satchel to blow us both to hell!"

I didn't look at him. I kept out of the light as much as possible, but I couldn't get off the road and leave tire tracks everywhere. When we neared the factory office building I cut sharply to the right and pulled around to the back. The car lights had been snapped off.

"Who's out there?" a voice called as I cut the motor.

"I thought this old man was deaf," Sheldon said.

"He's not so deaf that he can't hear eight cylinders charging down on him."

"What's his name?"

"Otto," I said. "Otto Finney."

And about that time the voice called again, "Who's that out there?"

"All right," Sheldon said, "you just sit here and watch the satchel. I'll be back in a minute."

I sat there feeling sweat popping out on my forehead. Sheldon seemed very cool as he got out of the car. He walked forward and called, "It's me, Otto."

"Who?"

"It's me," Sheldon called again.

I could see Otto now. When he opened the garage door a thin slice of light fell across the parking area in back of the building. The old man was standing in the light, holding a big hog-leg revolver in front of him. Sheldon kept walking toward him. "Can't you see a damn thing, Otto?" he said jokingly. "Don't you know who I am?"

"Oh," the old watchman said uncertainly. "Well..." Then he

let his revolver sag at his side. He still couldn't see a thing, standing in the light the way he was. Sheldon walked right up to him, and hit him.

That's all there was to it. I heard Sheldon's fist crack against the watchman's jaw, and then the old man's revolver clattered to the cement driveway, and he fell as though he had been shot. It was all very neat and clean and I felt weak with relief.

Sheldon dragged the old man inside the garage. I drove the Buick up against the building, in the shadows, then I got the satchel and Sheldon stuck his head through the doorway. "All right, Hooper. We can't take all night."

The garage was a big affair, almost as big as the warehouse itself, and the air was heavy with the smell of gasoline and oil. Four big trucks were parked in there and they seemed almost lost in the vastness of the place. A whisper could ricochet from one wall to another, building itself up until it sounded like a scream. "Over here, Hooper!" Sheldon called, and the loudness of his voice startled me.

The old watchman was as limp as a rag and pale as death, but there was only a trace of blood where Sheldon had hit him.

"Is he all right?" I asked.

"Sure he's all right. Now where is that master switch to the office building?"

I couldn't take my eyes off the old man. Sheldon already had him bound and gagged, but it looked like an unnecessary precaution to me. Otto Finney was dead! I would swear it! He lay there as still as any corpse I had ever seen, and his face had that yellowish cast that the dead or dying always have. As I stared at him I could feel the cold feet of panic walking right up my spine.

"He's dead!" I heard the words, but I didn't recognize the voice as mine.

"I told you he's all right," Sheldon said impatiently. "Now where is that switch?"

I wheeled on Sheldon with a kind of rage that I had never felt before. "You sonofabitch! He's dead! Do you think I don't know a dead man when I see one?" I went down on my knees and put my hand over the old man's heart.

I felt like a fool. The beat was there, as strong and steady as the tides.

"Are you satisfied?" Sheldon said dryly.

"All right, I'm sorry. The switch boxes are over on the west wall, over there by the workbenches. You want me to take care of it?"

Sheldon was all business. "You go back to the garage door and keep your eyes open. I probably know more about electrical wiring than you do. Besides, you don't want the old man waking up and recognizing you, do you?"

I hadn't even thought of that. I got out of there.

The minutes crawled by. Every minute seemed like an hour as I stood there in the darkness behind the garage with a thousand insane fears tearing through my brain. What if Sheldon fouled it up? What if he pulled the wrong switch, cut the wrong wire? What if the sky fell? What difference did it make? I was in it to my neck and there was no pulling out.

Then the lights went out. The garage was black. The whole building was black. But the lights were still on in the factory building across the way, and the floodlights were still on. I heard my breath whistling through my teeth in relief.

Sheldon had done the job right. Sheldon was a good man. At that moment I almost loved him. I heard him walking carefully across the cement floor of the garage, and then he was at the door.

"All right," he said, "I got the keys off the watchman. Let's go."

We went around to the far corner of the building, then under the catwalk, and walking into those floodlights was like walking into machine-gun fire. We cast shadows twenty feet long. We stood out like tarantulas in the snow.

"Jesus!" Sheldon said. We stood there blinking, our backs against the office building. I felt that if we walked under those lights they would be able to see us all the way to Tulsa. But there was absolutely no other way to do it. We had to go right up to that front door and open it.

"Well," Sheldon said finally, "at least we can be thankful that traffic is light on the highway."

"Give me the keys," I said.

Sheldon was still staring at that highway. "I'll take care of the door," he said at last. "You move back in the shadows and let me know the instant you spot a car. The first damn instant, understand?"

I was getting tired of being treated like an irresponsible idiot, but I kept telling myself that it wouldn't last much longer. I moved back against the wall, then went back to the catwalk and crossed over to the factory building, where I could stand in the shadows and still see the highway. Sheldon glanced at me and I nodded. He slipped around the corner and headed for the door.

He cast a shadow as big as an elephant against that brick wall. He went up the two cement steps to the door and I could hear the keys jingle as he went to work. I was so busy watching Sheldon that I didn't see the headlights on the highway until it was almost too late. Maybe it wouldn't have made any difference, maybe the people in the car wouldn't have noticed. But at that moment it seemed absolutely impossible that they could fail to notice Sheldon's enormous black shadow under the glare of those lights, and if they ever noticed, it was sure going to look fishy. People just don't fool around factories at that time of morning.

"Sheldon!" I called hoarsely.

He didn't hear me. He was so busy with that lock, concentrating so hard on which key to try, that he didn't hear a thing.

"Sheldon!" I practically yelled it this time, and this time he heard and reacted instantly. He hit the ground as though a bomb had gone off. He dropped off those steps, maybe three feet down, and hit face down in a flower bed. The car roared past the factory and hummed off into the night.

After a minute I gave him the go-ahead and he picked himself up and went back to work. It didn't take long. Not more than a lifetime. But he got the door open and motioned me to come on.

I crossed back over to the office building and sidled along the edge of that brick wall as though I were walking a tightrope. By the time I got inside, Sheldon was ready to go to work. It wasn't dark in there, with those floodlights pouring through the front windows, and Sheldon had already spotted the safe.

"Well," he said, sounding pleased, "this shouldn't be difficult." "

It still looked like a hell of a safe to me, but Sheldon was supposed to know. He was the expert.

"How long will it take?" I asked.

He shrugged, walking back and forth in front of the safe, looking it over from all angles. "That all depends. I'd say about fifteen minutes if I could use an electric drill, but I can't. As it is, it shouldn't take longer than thirty minutes."

That was going to be long enough for me. Already the echoing silence in the place was making me edgy. Sheldon was down on one knee, his black satchel open. He pulled on a pair of tight black suede gloves and tossed a pair of white cotton work gloves to me. "Put these on and wipe both doorknobs. Wipe the doorframe, too, while you're at it, and any other place that you think you might have touched."

By the time I had done that, Sheldon had his tools laid out—a hand-operated brace, diamond-tipped drilling bits, a teaspoon, a small bottle of yellowish liquid resting on a cushion of foam rubber.

"All right," I said, "what do I do now?"

"When I blow the door," he said, "we need to have something over the safe. Something like a very heavy quilt or blanket would do, but we'll have to make out with what we can find."

"How about a canvas tarp?" I said. "They usually keep them in the warehouse."

"Fine!" He locked in a drilling bit. "I couldn't have ordered anything better."

The warehouse was dark and ringing with silence. I could hear my own breathing, I could hear the wind sliding softly over the high tin roof. The echoes of my footsteps sounded like an army of marching men in the darkness.

I had no light, but I knew my way around back there, and I finally found the pile of heavy tarps that I was looking for. They were big pieces of canvas, maybe twenty feet square and very heavy. They used the tarps to protect new shipments of material from the weather when there wasn't enough storage room in the warehouse. The thing was too cumbersome to carry, so I dragged it across the cement floor and through the partition to Sheldon.

"How's it coming?" I said.

He just grunted. He had shed his coat and loosened his tie, and in the floodlight glow I could see the drops of sweat beaded on his forehead as he struggled with the brace and bit.

"Anything else you want me to do?" I asked.

"Just keep out of my way," he said shortly. "Go over to one of those windows and keep an eye on the highway. Don't bother me until I'm finished."

It looked like Sheldon's show from here on in. I went over to one of the far windows and stood staring out at the night. This was the part I didn't like. As long as I was too busy to think, it wasn't bad, but just standing and waiting began to get on my nerves. I began thinking about that Buick sitting outside. It was in the shadows, of course, hard against the building, but it would be a lot better if we could just open that big back door and drive it into the warehouse.

Then I began worrying about Otto Finney. What if the old man was really hurt? Hurt bad? What a hell of a mess that would be!

I looked at my watch and it was almost one-thirty. We had been there in the office almost forty minutes. What was taking Sheldon so long? Then I heard him throwing the tarp over the safe.

"You going to blow it?" I asked.

"That's what we came here for, isn't it?"

"You need any help?"

"All I need is for you to keep out of my way. Get over there by the partition and stay on your belly until this door's off."

I thought: One of these days I'm going to shove that nasty voice down your throat, Sheldon. But not now. I was going to be a good boy and do exactly as he said, because this was Sheldon's party.

"You ready?" he called.

"Yes."

"All right." He set the fuse, then took about five quick steps and lay down behind the safe. The building seemed to bulge with the explosion.

It wasn't such a loud noise—most of it was muffled by the tarp—but it was loud enough for me. It was enough to make the windows rattle. It was enough to make my teeth rattle, too.

But it did the job. The safe door flew open as though a

bomb had gone off inside, and a little whitish smoke drifted up in the darkness. Sheldon and I began picking ourselves up.

I couldn't be as casual about it as Sheldon was. I rushed to one window and then another, not knowing exactly what I expected to see, but something. It seemed impossible that nobody had heard that explosion. But evidently nobody had. Everything outside was nice and quiet, the highway empty. I began to breathe again.

When I got to the safe, Sheldon was grinning. "Well, here it is."

"It sure as hell is!" I had never seen so much money. The explosion must have broken the inside compartment, because money was scattered all over everywhere, nice new, clean, crisp, green bills, tens and twenties and fives and ones. It was beautiful.

I said, "What are we going to carry it in?"

"Carry it in the box it was in," Sheldon said. So we began crawling around on the floor, grabbing bills and stuffing them in the tin box. All that money! More money than I had ever dreamed of—and half of it was mine!

"Well," Sheldon said when we'd got it all together, "how does it feel to be rich?"

"It feels fine! But it will feel even better when we get away from this factory."

That was one time Sheldon gave me no argument. He got his satchel and I picked up the box of money, all that beautiful money, and we headed for the door.

We waited until the highway was clear and then made a run for it. Going under those floodlights was nothing now. I had thirty thousand dollars under one arm and was on top of the world. By the time we reached the garage I was four stories tall and growing by the minute.

"By God," Sheldon said, "I'll have to hand it to Manley. He said this would be a pushover, and it was. I'd never have believed there could be such a pushover if I hadn't seen it with my own eyes."

"Good old Manley!" I felt like laughing. "He's going to have a fit when he reads the morning paper."

"The hell with Manley," Sheldon said. "The sooner we get out of here, the better."

We had already started for the car when I heard it. I didn't know what it was, but it hit me like a hammer. Sheldon looked around at me. "What's the matter?"

"I don't know. I thought I heard something."

"Heard something? Where?"

"I don't know. I think it was in the garage." Both of us stood there as rigid as a pair of department-store dummies. I listened until my ears ached, every nerve drawn to the snapping point. Then it carne again, a scuffing, shoving sound that started an unscratchable itch on my scalp.

I glanced at Sheldon. "Did you hear it then?" He shook his head.

Maybe it was nothing. Maybe it was just an overactive imagination, or maybe it was just the strain. After all, a man doesn't commit a thirty-thousand-dollar robbery every day. But I had to be sure. It was much too late to begin taking chances.

I said, "Wait a minute. I want to have a look in there."

I opened the door and stepped into the pitch-darkness of the garage. There was no sound, absolutely no sound at all. Hooper, I thought, you'd better get hold of yourself before you go off the deep end. Then, just as I turned to go, the light hit me right in the face.

It was brighter than any light I had ever looked into. Brighter than those floodlights. Brighter than the sun. It hit me right in the eyes, that ball of brightness, and I couldn't see a thing. I lunged to one side just as the revolver crashed and resounded with unbelievable violence around the walls of that high garage. I felt the hot breath of the bullet. I heard the instantaneous spat! as the slug smashed itself against the brick wall.

I turned to run. I fell over something—God knows what —there in the darkness and went sprawling just as that revolver exploded again. Then I knew, somehow, instinctively, that running was not the answer.

That light had been on my face. The owner of that pistol was not only trying to shoot me, *he knew who I was!*

There was no time for rationalization. That deadly .38 of Sheldon's was in my hand. I fired once, twice, three times at the sweeping ball of light that was trying to pick me out of the darkness. I heard the incredible reverberations shatter the silence of the night, and I knew, somehow, that there was no use shooting any more.

It had happened with unbelievable speed. One second? Two seconds? No more than that. By the time Sheldon came crashing into the garage, it was all over.. Realization of what had happened was just beginning to hit me, and it left me cold and weak.

"Hooper!"

"It's all right," I heard myself saying. "It's all over." That flashlight still stabbed the darkness. I could hear it rocking back and forth on the cement floor. Its beam swept shorter and shorter arcs across the floor, and finally it stopped, pointing directly at me.

Sheldon said, "For God's sake, Hooper, what happened?"

"I just killed the watchman," I said.

## Chapter Seven

Sheldon took about four quick steps in front of me and picked up the flashlight. He turned the beam on the watchman's face.

He was dead, all right. There was no use feeling for a pulse this time. Those pale old eyes stared directly into the beam of light, unblinking. A broken little man, completely dead. He had fallen on a small heap of waste rags, the kind you find in every garage, and for a moment he looked as though he were another pile of rags and not a man at all.

Sheldon moved the flashlight beam up and down, slowly and carefully, and it was easy enough to see what had happened. The watchman's feet were still tied, but he had somehow managed to loosen his hands. He had pushed himself over to the garage wall, to a workbench where the pistol must have been, and the flashlight. Probably he was just beginning to untie his feet when I heard him.

Sheldon suddenly shot that beam of light at me. "Well, Hooper," he said tightly, "you've fixed things this time. You've fixed them good."

"I fixed them!" I stepped forward and knocked that beam out of my face. "You were supposed to have him tied and gagged! A fine fix we'd have been in if I hadn't stopped him before he threw that switch."

"Did you have to kill him?"

"What was I supposed to do? He had that flashlight right in my face!"

"But you didn't have to kill him. It could have been some other way."

Sheldon's voice was almost a whine now. I could look . right through that tough front of his and see his guts deserting him. This was something I hadn't figured on. If anybody went to pieces in this operation, I had expected it to be me. But I should have known. I'd seen the signs— I'd seen how Paula could shut him up. From personal experience I knew that he would not touch a job unless he figured it to be an absolute pushover. The signs were there, all right, but I hadn't seen them until it was too late.

Now Sheldon wiped his face on his coat sleeve. "This isn't just robbery now, it's murder! I didn't agree to anything like this."

"You didn't agree! Listen!" I grabbed the front of his shirt and twisted hard. "Listen to me! Do you think I wanted it? I liked this old man. I liked him a lot, and about the last thing in the world I'd want to do is kill him. But I had to do it. Do you hear me? He had the flashlight in my face!"

"Christ!" I could feel him shaking. "I didn't plan on anything like this!"

"You didn't plan! You gave me the gun, didn't you?"

It was amazing, really. I had never killed in my life and I had never imagined that it could be so easy. I was sorry that it had been Otto; it would worry me for a long time, but still it wasn't as bad as I had heard. It had been Otto or me. Otto had shot at me and I had shot back, and there was no way in the world to change it now. I had to accept it. Besides, there were other things to think about. It was staggering how many things there were.

"Hooper, we've got to get out of here!"

"Wait a minute. I think I've got something."

The one word that kept hitting me was "murder." To me it didn't have the usual meaning. It was like thinking of cancer or TB. You get yourself branded with it and it kills you, only with murder you the in the electric chair instead of in a bed.

I said, "Sheldon, you wait right here." Then I went down on one knee and lifted the dead watchman to my shoulder. Sheldon looked as though he had been clubbed. He stared dazedly as I hurried out of the garage with the dead man across my back. What I had in mind wasn't going to fool anybody for long, but it would cross the Sheriff up for a while, at least, and maybe that would be long enough.

It seemed, by now, that I had run that gantlet of floodlights a hundred times, but that didn't make it any easier this time. It was pure gambling; I just had to hope that no one saw me. Old Otto Finney had been a frail little man, and I was glad of that as I raced along the front of the building with him across my shoulders. I didn't even look at the highway. I went right up to the door, pressed Otto's palm to the latch and in two or three places along the door frame. Then I dragged him inside and did the same thing there. Finally I went over to the blown safe and made sure that Otto's fingerprints would be found on the door as well as other places.

That was that. I was breathing as though I had been swimming underwater, but I hoisted the dead man to my shoulders again and headed for the door. Just as I stepped outside I heard the sound of a motor, and then the headlights of a car cut a thin gash in the darkness of the highway. I hit the ground. The dead watchman hit and rolled a few feet ahead of me. As the car hummed past and out; of sight, I lay there for several seconds, breathing hard. And Otto was looking at me. Those pale, sightless eyes were wide open and staring right at me.

I said, "I'm sorry, Otto!" And I knew I had to get hold of myself or I was cooked. What was done was done. I wasn't going to crack up about it. That was the one thing in the world I couldn't afford to do. I shouldered the corpse and made another run for darkness.

Sheldon was right where I had left him, there by the garage door. I hadn't been afraid of his running out on me because I still had the key to the Buick. "Get the car door open," I panted. "The back seat."

By this time Sheldon had guessed what I was up to.

It won't work, Hooper," he said tightly.

"I know it won't work for long. But maybe it will buy us time, let the trail cool a little. Now get the door open."

He did it, and I dumped the dead watchman on the floor. Then the two of us went back to the garage and cleaned the place up. We picked up all the bloodstained rags, the gun, the flashlight. "Now," I said, "let's go!"

It was a long, long ride back to the tourist court; I hope I never take another ride as long as that one. Every car I met I expected to be the Sheriffs car. I expected something violent to happen every second, but nothing did. Nothing happened at all. What we were going to do with the dead watchman, I didn't know. I was beyond thinking. It took all my concentration just to keep the car in a straight line.

Then at last we reached the cabins, and I pulled the Buick

behind the station and into the carport next to Number 2. There were no lights in the cabin, but Paula had the door open the minute we pulled off the highway, and she was right there the second we hit the carport.

She jerked the door open on my side.

"What took you so long? Did anything go wrong?"

I could smell the perfume she wore. Or maybe it wasn't perfume, maybe it was just her.

"Something happened, didn't it?" she said. "Tell me!"

Sheldon hadn't said a thing. But now he turned toward his wife, and his face looked a hundred years old. "The trouble," he said, "is back there."

Paula opened the back door and made one small sound when she saw the dead man. Then she looked at me.

"Who did it?"

"I did."

She frowned. "I might have known it couldn't have been Karl."

"I guess we need to talk this thing over," I said, and got out of the car.

Sheldon sat where he was. "Paula," he said, "we've got to get out of here. Get your things together right now."

"The three of us?" she asked coldly, glancing at the back seat.

"Oh." He looked pretty foolish and he knew it, and that did more than anything else to snap him out of it. "Well, maybe Hooper's right, maybe we should talk it over, coolly, calmly."

There was a moon out that night. I didn't notice it until I got inside the darkened cabin and saw the whitish moonlight pouring through the open door. "Turn the light on," Paula said.

"It will be safer if we don't," I said.

"We can't count the money in the dark."

First things first. I felt a crazy impulse to laugh. The hell with the dead man outside, we had money to count. She turned the light on.

It really didn't make much difference. The cabins, as usual, were empty, and I was too tired to care, anyway. I was having trouble keeping my thoughts organized.

Then I thought: Christ, I've forgotten all about the money! I kicked the door open, went out to the car, and got it. I didn't look behind the front seat; I didn't want to see those pale, wide eyes again. Just don't think about it, I thought. He asked for it, didn't he?

Paula's eyes were alive with excitement as she dug her hands into the green bills. "Thirty thousand dollars!"

Sheldon said, "We don't know how much there is. We haven't, counted it."

"I can tell! Just by feeling of it!"

"For God's sake," I said, "stop playing with the stuff and let's count it!"

Then Paula turned on me with a tight little smile. "First," she said, "tell me about the watchman." The look in her eyes shook me. "Forget it," I said. All this talk was rubbing right through to my nerves. "The old man shot at me and I had to kill him. That's all there was to it."

"I knew it!" She almost sneered, looking now at Sheldon. "I knew it couldn't have been you, Karl!"

I didn't know what she was talking about, but Sheldon must have. He stood rigid for just a moment, his eyes stormy, and then, without a sound of warning, he back-handed her. The back of his fist slammed into her mouth, knocking her across the room and onto the bed. "Now keep quiet, goddamn you!" he said hoarsely.

I felt the muscles become tense in my shoulders. Stay out of it, I warned myself. This is between just the two of them. You can't afford to butt in now—not until we make the split, anyway.

His knuckles had broken Paula's lower lip and a thin little stream of blood dripped down her chin. She didn't come fighting back, as I had thought she would. She felt of her lip. Then she opened a suitcase, took out some paper tissue, and held it to her mouth. She didn't say a word, but there was plenty in her eyes. Sheldon dumped the money on the table and began counting it out. I helped him. It came to $31,042. We cut it right down the middle without a word: $15,521 each. "Not bad," Sheldon said. "If we live long enough to spend it!" "Oh, yes," Sheldon said softly, as though he had been trying to forget it too. "The body."

I glanced at Paula and she was still sitting exactly the way she had been for fifteen minutes, there on the edge of the bed, holding the bloody tissue to her mouth. Now she stood up and

I could see that all the fight hadn't been knocked out of her.

"Why did you bring the body with you, anyway?" "Because," I said, "I went to a good deal of trouble putting the watchman's fingerprints all over the safe before we left the factory."

"Oh." She was getting it now, but I stopped her before she had a chance to carry it too far.

"Don't get the idea," I said, "that the Sheriffs going to be fooled. He's not going to think for one damn minute that Otto Finney robbed that factory. Still, the evidence is going to be there and he's going to have to look into it. And if we can get rid of the body, the Sheriff is going to have to look for it, and that's going to take time."

"Time for us to get far away from Oklahoma," Sheldon said softly. "Well, the rest is up to you, Hooper. What do we do with the body?"

That question had been drumming at me ever since I pulled the trigger. So far, I had been pretty successful in keeping it impersonal. I tried to think of it as a problem to be solved, and nothing else. "The lake," I said. "It's the only thing I can think of. Drop the body in the lake."

Sheldon frowned. "Tell me about this lake."

"Creston's water supply, a man-made affair about four miles out of town. There's a deep hole at the north end that would give them plenty of trouble if they tried to drag. Anyway, there are a lot of garfish in that water, and I doubt if a body would be recognized after a day or two, even if they got it up."

Keep it impersonal, I reminded myself. But the thought of those scavenger fish wasn't pleasant.

Sheldon turned it over in his mind. "All right, that's the way it will have to be. We haven't got time to think of something better."

I shook my head. "There's something else about this lake that you'd better know about. It's kind of like a local lovers' lane. When couples don't have anywhere else to go, they head for the lake."

"At this time of night?"

"At *any* time of night. That's what I'm trying to tell you. There's just a chance we might be seen."

"Then the lake's out," Sheldon said shortly.

"The lake's all we have," I reminded him. "Paula could go

with me; the two of us could handle it. If we happen to be seen, nobody's likely to give it a second thought." Time was running out and I had to talk to Paula. This was the only way I could think of doing it.

Sheldon didn't like it, but this was no time to smooth out the rough places. What Paula thought about it she didn't say. The three of us stood there, looking at each other, and then I said, "I'll be back in a minute." I gathered up my half of the money and went out.

I put the money under the mattress in my cabin, and then I went to the station and rummaged around in the darkness until I found what I wanted—a cast-off flywheel and a set of rusty mud chains. I was working smoothly now.

Just keep cool, I thought, and everything is going to work out all right. Then I went back to the Buick to put the wheel and chains in the back seat.

About a minute later Sheldon came out. "What's the matter?"

"Nothing. We've got to move the body to my car, though. I can't afford to be seen in this Buick."

"Hooper, are you sure this lake business is all right?"

"Can you think of anything better?"

He wasn't worried about the lake, he was worried about Paula. But he merely shrugged. Between the two of us we got the old watchman's body into the back seat of my Chevy and covered it with a piece of canvas from the station. Then we loaded the flywheel and chains and everything was set—as set as it would ever be. I looked at my watch and it was almost three o'clock.


The thing went like clockwork. There was just enough moon to make driving without lights possible on that twisting lake road. The place was deserted, not a car, not a soul anywhere, and the lake itself was motionless. Not a ripple was on the water. When I reached the spot I was looking for, I drove on for maybe a mile to make sure that the way was completely clear, and then I turned around and came back.

It was just as I had remembered it, shelves of brownish rock jutting out of a red clay bank, and below it the lake. I knew how deep it was there, for as a kid I had seen the bulldozers gouging it out. There was no need of a boat, no need of taking the body out to the middle of the lake before dumping it. Just drop it over that shelf of rock and let the lake settle over it and keep it forever and ever, amen. He was an old man, I thought. He wouldn't have lived much longer anyway. "Is this the place?" Paula said. "Yes."

I got out of the car and lugged the chains and flywheel over to the edge of the rock. Then I went back to the car and carried the body—the amazingly light, frail old body —over to the rock and put it down. I then slipped the chains through the flywheel and fastened the other end of chain to the body with several pieces of strong wire.

"Can I help?" Paula said.

"No." I eased the dead watchman over the ledge, then gave the flywheel a shove, and there was a silvery splash as the body and weight plunged down and down, and I stood there watching as they sank out of sight.

"Good!" Paula said huskily. She looked as soft and pale as the moonlight. I knew we should get away from there as fast as possible, but there were still some things to get settled. I wasn't fool enough to think the killing hadn't changed things. I couldn't possibly just pack up and leave with Paula; that would look too fishy now, right after the robbery. But she was in my blood and something had to be worked out.

I walked over to her and she stood there looking at me with that tight little smile at the corners of her swollen mouth. Then she reached out and touched my shoulder, and she said, "You've got guts, Joe Hooper."

Staying there was idiocy, but I couldn't seem to move.

"I like a man with guts," she said huskily. "I like a man to be strong."

"What about your husband?"

She made a small sound. "Karl spent a long stretch in Leavenworth, and—do you know why? Because he was afraid to pull the trigger. He let the cops take him because he was afraid to shoot."

"That isn't what I meant. What do we do now, you and me?"

Like a lusty young animal, she wrapped those white arms around me. She was fire in my arms. The taste of blood was in my mouth when I kissed her.

"What do you want to do, Joe? About us."

"I want to hold you just like this and never let you go. But that's impossible now. Within a few hours cops are going to be swarming all over this part of the country, and they're going to be asking a hell of a lot of questions."

"Then you want me to go tonight with Karl?"

"It looks like the only thing for the present. How can I get in touch with you as soon as things cool off here?"

She thought for a moment. "I have a sister in Missouri. Mrs. Stella Bundy, Box Three-forty, Route Three, St. John, Missouri. She'll know how to find me. Can you remember the address?"

## Chapter Eight

It was almost five o'clock when we got back to the cabins and Sheldon was fit to be tied. He grabbed his wife and jerked her out of the car as though she were a bag of groceries. "Goddamn you!" he snarled. "Where have you been?"

He looked as though he were going to tear her head off and she just smiled. "Don't get excited, Karl. You know where we've been."

He knew where she had been, all right. Or he was guessing pretty close to it. A family ruckus was the last thing in the world I wanted right now, and I didn't like the ugliness in his voice. I stepped out of the car and said, "Did you ever try to get rid of a body, Sheldon? You don't just dump it in a gully. You have to do it exactly right or it's too damn bad. I didn't know it was going to take this long, but it did, and there's nothing we can do about it."

Glaring at me, he took one deep breath, then he flung his wife against the side of the car and went into the cabin. "Well!" Paula said softly. "You'd almost think he was a man, wouldn't you, when he's mad?"

I said nothing. The sky along the eastern edge of the prairie was beginning to pale, and I could feel all the strength going out of me. I felt a hundred years old. I didn't let myself think about the things that would start happening within the next few hours. That robbery was going to turn Creston upside down and shake it, and I just hoped that I would be able to ride it out.

Then Sheldon came out with the luggage. He threw it into the car without a word and Paula glanced at me and shrugged. "Maybe we'll meet again, Mr. Hooper," she said dryly.

She smiled again and slipped onto the front seat beside her husband. Karl Sheldon looked at me once. He didn't say a word, he just sat there and looked at me with all the hate that was in him. Then, with one savage movement, he jammed the Buick into gear and they were on their way.

I stood there for maybe five minutes. I watched as the Buick slammed violently onto the highway, spewing gravel and dust into the still morning air, and I listened with relief as the car dropped behind a small rise and the roar became a drone, and the drone became a hum, and the hum became nothing. Silence.

Strangely, I felt nothing. I stood there and the pale sky became suddenly bloody as the violent sun lifted into a widening sky. Finally I turned and walked to my own cabin.

There was no use going to sleep. I had to open the station within an hour, because I always opened the station at six-thirty in the morning, and this morning had to be exactly like all the others. I made a pot of coffee, black as evil, strong as temptation, and I sat at the tiny kitchen table and watched that savage sun begin its violent work. Even my bones ached with weariness. I looked at my watch and it was nearly six, so I turned on the light and went to the bathroom to shave.

My face looked back at me from the bathroom mirror, and nothing could have shocked me more. It seemed incredible that I could have survived such a night without changing, but there was no change at all. The face was mine. The eyes seemed faintly tired, but no more so than they often did in the morning. I don't know just what I expected to see in that mirror, but the sight of my own unchanged face almost made me sick.

This is fine! I thought bitterly as I lathered to shave. Just a little more of this and you're cooked, Hooper. Get a hold on yourself, and you'd better be damn sure you keep it.

I felt a little better after the shave. Then I stripped and showered and got into my work clothes—and only then did I remember the money. I grabbed the mattress and threw it to the floor.

The money was still there. I took it in my hands. The bills were crisp to my touch. The smell of ink and silk-fibered paper was like the smell of roast beef to a starving man.

For a while I had trouble thinking of a place to put the money. The woman who cleaned the cabins might run across it if I left it here, so I took it to the station with me when I opened up. The first thing I did was wrap the money in clean waste; then I moved several cases of oil and loosened a plank in the flooring. That's where the money went, under the floor, and the cases of oil went back on top of it. That would have to do until I thought of something better.

I felt all right now. It was almost seven o'clock by the time

I'd finished unlocking the gas pumps and connected the hose for water and air. The tourists were already beginning to hit the highway, getting an early start on the heat. I went back into the station and turned on the radio.

"... between midnight and four in the morning, according to the authorities," the announcer was saying. "No details are available as yet, but it is believed that the entire Provo Box Company payroll was taken in the robbery. Otis Miller, Creston County sheriff, has issued no statement concerning the disappearance of Otto Finney, the factory's watchman. The robbery was discovered less than an hour ago, when Paul Killman, shop foreman, delivered a company truck to the garage...."

They knew nothing. They weren't even sure how much money had been taken.

By noon they knew a little more, but not much. "It is not known whether more than one person took part in the robbery, but it has been determined that entry to the company's office was made possible by use of a key —probably the key that Watchman Otto Finney kept on his person. Also, it was learned that the factory's burglar-alarm system was rendered ineffectual by a circuit break at the master switch box in the garage. This has led to speculation that the burglar or burglars must have been familiar with the factory layout, and it has been suggested, off the record, that an employee of the Provo Box Company may soon be named as a suspect. However, Sheriff Otis Miller claims he suspects no one at the present time, although the watchman was still missing as we went on the air. Ray King, Miller's deputy, said this morning that several fingerprints were found on and near the blown safe and that these will be checked...." I could smile. The Sheriff knew as well as I did that Otto Finney had nothing to do with the robbery, but pressure for investigation was being brought down on him and he would have to look into it. While the real trail grew colder, And colder. By the time they permitted Otis to stop chasing his tail, there would be no trail at all.

It was exactly the way I had figured it. But there was small satisfaction in it for me. I was too sick with fatigue to feel satisfaction or anything else. All I wanted right now was for Ike Abrams to relieve me and give me a chance to get some sleep.

And that was the day Ike had to be late. It was almost one o'clock when that Ford of his rattled off the highway.

"Where the hell have you been?" I said. "It's almost one and I haven't even had lunch yet."

He was a lanky, easygoing guy, but that day there was excitement in his sleepy eyes. "By God, hell's bustin' loose in town, Joe! I guess I forgot what time it was. You heard about the robbery, didn't you?"

"The box factory? It was on the radio."

"Well, it's the damnedest thing you ever saw, the way it's got the town boilin'."

I was too tired to care, but I couldn't walk off without showing a normal amount of interest. "I figured most people hated Max Provo's guts," I said. "Why should they get worked up because he lost some money?"

"It ain't Provo that bothers them, it's old Otto Finney. Half of them say he ought to be caught and lynched. They claim old Otto's the only one could have done it, him having the keys and knowing about the burglar alarm and all. And the other half claim the old man's probably dead somewhere, wherever the burglars buried him after they killed him."

"And what do you think, Ike?"

Ike shrugged. "Old Otto never cared about money. He never showed it, anyway. But it's goin' to look bad if those fingerprints on the safe turn out to be his."

"Has the Sheriff got any clues besides the fingerprints?"

Ike grinned faintly. "Otis ain't talking. Half the City Council is pullin' him one way, half the other."

Just the way I had planned it. I was pleased. "I wouldn't want to be in the Sheriff's shoes," I said.

And Ike said, "I wouldn't want to be in the *burglar's* shoes. The harder they make it on Otis, the more determined he'll be to catch them. And he'll do it, too. In spite of the City Council or anybody else."

I rubbed my face, only half hearing what Ike said. "Well," I said, "it's the Sheriff's baby, not mine."

I went to my cabin, too tired even to wash my face and hands. I dropped on the bed and began to sweat in that blistering heat. Almost immediately unconsciousness began closing in like a steaming blanket.

And it was night again.

And there we were, Sheldon and I, racing under the blinding brilliance of floodlights. It was an endless, vacant avenue lighted by a thousand suns, and we were racing up that dazzling stretch where there was no sound, no shadow. That was the thing I noticed, there was no shadow. Just Sheldon and I racing through that shocking brilliance. There was a heavy load on my shoulders. I felt myself falling and I called out to Sheldon but he did not hear. He continued to run, and the load on my shoulders bore me down. Now it seemed that all the lights, every dazzling little sun, turned upon me as I fell. The load was suddenly lifted from my shoulders as I struck the ground, and I lay there for a long while, breathless, as the gathering suns watched and waited. And that was when I saw the eyes, two old eyes, very old and very dead, and they were staring right at me. I awoke staring into the brilliance of the sun, the real sun. Its furnace-like heat reached through the cabin window and struck my face.

I rolled over and lay drunkenly on the soggy bed. The dream was still with me and the terror of it was in the room. Automatically, I shoved myself up from the bed. I stumbled to the bathroom and washed my face. I sloshed cold water on the back of my neck until I was fully awake.

I stood there for a long while, rigidly, waiting for the lingering terror of the dream to slip away. I soaked a towel and wrapped it around my neck, and then I went to the bedroom and then into the kitchen, touching things as I passed in an effort to prove to myself that I was awake and that the dream was gone.

I opened a can of beer and went to the bedroom. A strange thing happened then—or perhaps it wouldn't seem so strange to people who knew about such things. I began to hate Otto Finney.

It came slowly at first, and then with a rush, and within a matter of minutes I hated the old watchman more man I had ever hated a man in my life. I was *glad* he was dead. I was *glad* I had killed him. In my mind I had a completely new picture of what had happened, and now Otto was the villain, not I.

I don't know.... Maybe it's what a psychiatrist would call "defense mechanism." Maybe they would say that turning my hate on Otto was an attempt to "justify my crime." I don't know....

I only know that hate came when I needed it most. It saved my sanity.

Killing a man was not so difficult—I had learned that. But to go on liking him is not compatible with sanity—I had learned that, too. Killing and hatred are brothers. They go together, they are inseparable. If one is missing, it must be created from what is at hand.

And so it was.

But it came slowly at first. I thought: It should never have happened. If he hadn't shone that flashlight in Any face, it never would have happened. If he hadn't shot at me, it never would have happened.

And the inevitable tangent to this circle of thought was: He had no right to shoot at me! I wasn't trying to take his money! But he had shot at me. He had tried to kill me. Goddamn him, the whole thing could have been so easy and simple. A pushover, Sheldon had called it. But that watchman had to be a hero, he had to try to ruin everything just at the last minute.

And so hate was created. At the time, of course, I did not look at it objectively and I did not question it. The terror of the dream was too close for objectivity. I welcomed my new hate and held it close. I thought, I'm *glad* I killed him!

If it is true that hate is a defense mechanism, it is an effective one. It stands head and shoulders above fear. And it has strength, that's the important thing. I could feel myself growing stronger, and it was good to know that I would be able to sleep again and not dream.

The hell with Otto Finney!

## Chapter Nine

The Sheriff's office was in the courthouse basement. I walked down the corridor of dirty marble and was almost sick at the steaming smell of unemptied spittoons and filthy toilets and stale cigar smoke, and I wondered why it was that the sheriffs office was always in the basement, and why it was that small-town courthouses were always so filthy. Near the end of the corridor there was a sign that said: "Otis Miller, Sheriff."

Ray King was sitting at a desk just inside the front office. "Well, Joe, what brings you down to the courthouse?"

"Hello, Ray. I'd like to see Otis, if he's around."

"Sheriffs tied up right now, in the back office. He ought to be free in a minute. Take a chair."

I sat down in a straight-backed hard-oak chair, hoping that coming to the Sheriff wasn't a mistake. Mistake or not, I felt that it would be a good idea if I could find out what Otis thought about the robbery. It had been three days now and the papers had printed the same thing over and over again, and the Sheriff had said nothing, nothing at all, and there was no way of telling what he was thinking or doing. And I had to know. Before I could think of contacting Paula, I had to know.

Ray sat there grinning for a few seconds, then he pulled some papers in front of him and picked up a pen. "Excuse me a minute, Joe. Otis will be on my back if I don't get this report finished."

"Sure. Sure."

There was nothing else to do, so I sat back and tried to ignore the heat and watched Ray working on the white form. He didn't look much like a deputy sheriff, but the business was in his blood and it was more or less taken for granted that he would get Otis Miller's job when Otis decided it was time to step down. Ray's dad had been a U.S. marshal when Creston was just a stage stop in Oklahoma Territory, and there was a stone monument out west of town marking the place where he had been killed in a gun fight with two Territory badmen.

So it was natural enough that Ray should take up the law-enforcing business, although he looked pretty light for that kind of work. He was a lanky, easygoing sort of guy, not much older than myself. He looked more like a lawyer or a businessman than a deputy sheriff. Most of the time, when it wasn't too hot, he wore a dark, double-breasted suit. No cowboy boots and white hat for Ray King, and he never wore his gun where it would show, but he knew the business of a sheriff as well as Otis Miller did.

Maybe ten minutes passed, and finally an inner door opened and out came Pat Sully, the guy I'd paid that five dollars to that day at the box factory. That jarred me for a moment. Surely Pat hadn't suspected me! The big red-faced bastard was too dumb to put two and two together.

Still, it was something to think about. It turned me cold for just a moment, until. I heard Sully say, "I hope I've been some help, Sheriff."

Otis Miller followed him out. "Well, we can't tell about that, Pat, until we put all the pieces together. 'I've called in everybody on old Provo's office force on the long chance that they might know something." Then they shook hands and Pat turned to leave.

He saw me then. "Why, hello, Joe. What are you doing in this part of town?"

"Got a little business with the Sheriff, nothing important. How are things out at the box factory?"

Sully shook his head. "It's a mess. You never saw such a mess in your life. Old Provo's fit to be tied about this robbery." He grinned faintly. "Well, I guess I'd better get back to it."

I breathed easier. Nothing to worry about, I told myself. The Sheriff's talking to the entire office force. A matter of routine.

The Sheriff looked at me and I could see the tight little lines around the corners of his mouth. They were putting the pressure on him, all right.

"You waitin' to see me, Joe?"

"If you're not too busy, Sheriff. It's about that bogus bill I took in."

"Oh." He rubbed his face and I could see that he was annoyed. "Well, all right," he said after a second. "Come on in the office."

The Sheriff was a short, squat barrel of a man. He wore

cowboy boots and the pants and vest of a blue serge suit. He had a big pearl-handled .45 that he wore cowboy style on his right hip, even in the office. Looking at Otis Miller for the first time, you'd think that here was just another small-town politician who had seen too many Buck Jones movies, full of wind and nothing else. You couldn't be more wrong. Otis Miller was as tough as steer hide, and his reputation as a lawman was spotless.

He planted himself behind his desk, as solid as an oak stump. "Well," he said, "let's see it."

I gave him the bill and he held it up to the light.

"You've got stuck, all right."

"It looks like it," I said. "I guess there's not much to be done about it now," wondering how I was going to get around to the robbery.

Otis was still squinting at the bill. "When did you say you got this?"

"Four or five days ago. I found it in my cash drawer."

He grunted. Then he got up and went to a small office safe in the corner of the room. He took another bill from the safe and held them up to the window. "I'm no expert," he said finally, "but I'd swear these two bills came off the same press." He handed them to me. "Look at the scrollwork in the upper left-hand corners."

I held the two bills up to the light, and sure enough, they were exactly the same. The same engraving flaws were in both bills. "Where did this one come from?" I said, holding out the bill he had given me.

He shrugged. "Don't remember exactly. Several of them were passed here in Creston about a year ago. Directly after that the counterfeiters were caught in Tulsa."

Otis was looking at me. It was just a look, I told myself, and didn't mean a thing, but I felt that chill again.

"They were caught?" It was all I could think to say.

"A year ago. They're in Leavenworth now."

"How about me plates?"

"They were taken, too. They were so bad that the counterfeiters had stopped using them." The Sheriff dropped the bill and let it flutter to his desk. "Very few of these bills were passed," he said thoughtfully, "according to the federal men who were on the case. Look at them. That kind of work wouldn't fool an idiot—no offense, Joe."

Goddamnit! I thought. Why did I ever think of this bogus bill, anyway? "Well..." I didn't like the way he was looking at me. "Where do you figure this bill came from?"

He shrugged.

"Somebody must have held onto it for a year and then passed it off on me."

"It's possible," Otis said.

But not probable. Bogus money as bad as this stuff just didn't stay in circulation. I couldn't tell what he was thinking, if he was thinking anything. He just looked at me and fingered that bogus bill.

"Then," I said, "I guess there's nothing much we can do about it, if the counterfeiters are already in prison."

He smiled faintly. "Maybe the experience will be worth five dollars to you, Joe. From now on you'll look at your bills before ringing them up."

I had an almost irresistible impulse to wipe the sweat from my forehead. It was nothing. I was just imagining things. The Sheriff said, "Was there anything else on your mind, Joe?"

"No. No, that's all," and got up. "I guess this robbery thing has got you pretty busy," I added.

"Yes. In fact, there are some people I want to talk to right now. So if you don't mind ..."

That was a dismissal. He stood up and hitched his holster. "Well, take it easy, Joe," and he walked out of the office.


I hadn't learned a thing. That didn't occur to me until I had reached the sidewalk in front of the courthouse. I had been on the defensive every minute; I hadn't had a chance to ask questions.

I was tempted to go back and talk to Ray King and see if I could get anything out of him, but that would be too risky. If Otis did get to wondering about that bogus bill, everything I did would begin to mean something to him. He was a bulldog when he got hold of a thing. Let well enough alone, I told myself. Give Otis no reason to believe that I tried to fool him with that piece of counterfeit and everything will be all right.

I looked at my watch and it was three o'clock. Three days, almost four, since the robbery, since I had seen Paula. It seemed like a lifetime.

Across the street from the courthouse there was a bar, and that's where I headed. I stood there with my foot on the rail for maybe fifteen minutes, nursing a schooner of beer and wondering what I was going to do next. I was free; Ike was taking care of the station for the afternoon. Free to visit with my dad, free to do anything I wanted, and I wanted to do nothing. I didn't even want the beer. Then a paper boy came in with the afternoon paper, the only paper Creston had, and I took one. It was in the headlines.

## FINGERPRINTS ON PROVO SAFE

### IDENTIFIED AS MISSING WATCHMAN'S

Otis Miller, Creston County sheriff, said this morning that the fingerprints found on the blown door of the Provo Box Company safe had definitely been identified as those of Otto Finney, missing company watchman. Finney has been missing since the night of the robbery....

I read it and felt myself smile. The paper, without coming right out and saying it, made it sound like an open-and-shut case against Otto. Now I knew why the Sheriff had been annoyed at my bothering him with that bogus bill. He knew perfectly well that the old watchman was innocent, but that wouldn't keep the political wolves off his back. There was only one thing for him to do, and that was to find Otto. By the time he did that, if he ever did, the details of the case would be so fogged that the trail would never be picked up again.

Suddenly I felt good. I felt fine. I had another schooner of beer and this time I enjoyed it. It was strange, the way that story in the paper affected me. It was difficult to believe that it had anything to do with me, anything at all. A factory had been robbed. An old watchman was missing. That was all. I could even think back to the night when Paula Sheldon and I had dumped the body over the rock ledge into the lake and feel nothing but a kind of cold savagery. The old bastard had tried to kill me! He got what was coming to him!

I had another beer, and this time the bartender leaned over the bar to look at the paper. "Well, I'll be damned," he said. "That makes it look bad for old Finney, don't it? But you want to know what I think? I think the old man's dead."

I looked at him. "Why?"

"Just a hunch, maybe." He shrugged. "That's the way I've got it figured, though. I've been thinking about this thing, and I just don't believe the old man could have done it. I don't give a damn about the fingerprints. I think the robbers killed him and dumped his body in the lake."

I must have jumped.

"What's the matter?" he said. "You look kind of funny."

"Nothing's the matter. But what made you think of the lake?"

"Well, it just seems like the logical place to me. I ask myself how would be the best way to get rid of a body in a hurry, and I think right away of the lake. I don't know why; it's just the obvious place, I guess."

It was obvious, if this stupid bartender had thought of it. Dangerously obvious.

"It's my guess," he went on, "that the Sheriff would be dragging the lake right now if he could get the officials together on it. There are too many damn fools in town, though, that think the old man actually took part in the burglary and is hidin' out somewhere. But they'll come around in time. Then you'll see I'm right."

I wanted to get out of there. I was beginning to realize that the lake hadn't been such a fine idea after all, and if it weren't for the wrangle in the City Council I'd be in a hell of a mess. I said, "Well, I guess the Sheriff knows what he's doing."

"Sure, if they'd just let him do it. You know, I've got another theory about this thing. I'll bet somebody right here in Creston took that money and killed Finney. Otis Miller will get them, though. I'll bet on it."

I downed the beer and got out of there. I'd heard enough.

I got back to the station around sundown and Ike Abrams

said, "Anything new in town?"

"Not much. I talked to the Sheriff about the counterfeit bill. We'll have to chalk it up to experience."

"I heard on the radio that the fingerprints on the safe belonged to Otto Finney. That's hard to believe, isn't it?"

"You can't ever tell about people, I guess. Anything new out here?"

"Everything's about the same." Then he grinned. "By , golly, there is something. You remember the guy with the blonde wife, the ones in the blue Buick?"

An anvil dropped in my stomach.

"Well," Ike said, "they're back."

## Chapter Ten

I couldn't believe it. It was impossible! They couldn't be stupid enough to come back here at a time like this!

But they had. That blue Buick was parked in the carport beside Number 2, like the returning of a nightmare. "I don't know what we've got," Ike said, "but they must like it. This is the third time they've stopped here, isn't it?"

"I don't remember."

"Sure, two times before. I remember the last time was the night the box factory was robbed."

I was about to blow up. Why had they come back? "Maybe you're right," I said, and my voice was surprisingly calm. I felt like yelling.

"You goin' to town tonight?" Ike asked.

"No. There's no need of your staying on; I'll close the station myself."

"I don't mind staying."

"Ike, take the night off. I want to go over the books, anyway." He stood there grinning, and I could have slugged him. "What's the matter with you? What are you grinning at?"

"Why, nothing, I guess. Is anything wrong?"

"No, nothing's wrong. Go on, Ike, take the night off."

"Whatever you say, Joe."

I was tingling all over. I wanted to get that Sheldon by the throat and beat some sense into his stupid skull. And Ike wouldn't leave. He kept puttering around for maybe five minutes while I tried to keep from yelling.

"Well, if you're sure you won't need me tonight..." he said finally.

"I won't need you, Ike. That's the truth."

I was as tight as a drum. Just about another minute of Ike and I would have exploded. But he left. I was never so glad to get rid of anybody in my life.

Now that he was gone, I didn't know what to do. I had to see Sheldon. I had to find out if he had completely lost his mind. He must have lost his mind, coming back here at a time like this! At least Paula should have known better.

I was afraid to leave the station untended, but it looked like the only way. As soon as Ike was out of sight, I headed for Number 2. There was a coldness inside me; I was ready to take somebody's throat in my hands and start squeezing.

Paula was at the door when I got there, and the sight of her jarred me. She looked as though she hadn't slept for a week. That blonde hair wasn't as blonde as it had been before, and it looked as though it hadn't been combed since the night of the robbery. I jerked the door open and said, "What the hell do you mean, coming back here?"

She took two steps back, like a sleepwalker, and glanced at the bed. Sheldon was stretched out on the covers, his face flushed, his lips tight. One shirt sleeve had been ripped off at the shoulder and his left arm was bound with what looked to be dirty rags.

"Hooper?" he almost whispered.

"Goddamn you, why did you—"

"I've got to have a doctor," he said, talking through clenched teeth.

I wheeled on Paula, who still hadn't made a sound. "What's wrong with him?"

She smiled then, without humor. "He's been shot."

The full implications still didn't hit me. "How did it happen?"

"We'll go into that later."

"We'll go into it now!"

She shrugged. "All right We were in Texas. We saw this drugstore, a little hick drugstore in a little one-horse town in Texas. I was buying some aspirin and I saw the druggist go to the safe, and I saw the money there. It looked easy." She sighed wearily. "There must have been a week's take there in a safe that I could have opened myself."

"And then what happened?"

"For God's sake," Sheldon said hoarsely, "don't stand there talking. I've got to have a doctor!"

"And then what happened?" I said again.

Again Paula smiled that smile that wasn't a smile at all. "We took the drugstore that night. Or we almost did. The town marshal, a hick town marshal, just happened to see us as we were leaving. The whole town was asleep, but not that hick marshal. He was a hero. He had been wearing that six-shooter for God knows how long, just waiting for a chance to use it. And he used it oil Karl."

"But why come here, all the way from Texas?"

"Karl's got blood poisoning, I think."

"But why did you come here?" I insisted. She sank to a chair beside the kitchen table.

"Because," she said, "Karl has to have a doctor. And because doctors don't treat gunshot wounds without reporting them. And," she added, "because I remembered that your father was a doctor and I thought maybe he would overlook the report if it was for a friend of yours."

That stunned me. It had been obvious all the time, but she had to spell it out for me before I got it.

"You're crazy!"

She shrugged, very lightly.

"You must be insane," I almost yelled. "Or maybe you just don't know what an honest man is like. Well, that's what my father is. Nothing in the world could make him take a case like this and not report it!"

"Not even to save his son from the electric chair?"

She had me.

She knew she had me, and she could start turning the screw any time she felt like it. And she felt like it right now. She stood up suddenly, and she didn't look so tired now. She pushed her hair back and looked straight at me with those cool blue eyes. "I'm not going to argue about this. Karl has to have a doctor."

"Then get one of your own!"

"You know that's impossible. Your father is the doctor we want, the one we're going to have."

And then a car honked outside and the sound made me jump.

"What's that?" Her eyes brightened just a little.

"Somebody at the station. A customer. I've got to get back."

"Have you got a telephone at the station?"

"No."

The corners of her mouth turned up again. "Sure you have. Well, call your father and tell him to get out here, understand?"

The car honked again and we stood there staring at each other, and even then, at a time like that, I kept thinking what a hell of a woman she was. She had looks, she had brains, and she could set a man on fire. I hated her guts at that moment, and it was all I could do to keep my hands off her.

"For God's sake!" Sheldon groaned.

"You'd better go, Joe," she said, and fatigue crept back into her face. I turned on my heel. "And don't forget to call your father," she added as I went out the door.

I was shaking with rage when I got back to the station. The guy was just beginning to honk the horn again as I rounded the corner. "All right!" I yelled. *"All right!"*

They were tourists, a fat old geezer of about sixty and a little pinch-faced woman. I looked in the car window and said, "Fill her up?"

"No, we just want a cabin," the man said.

Of all the times to get business! "I'm sorry," I said, "we're full up."

"You've got a 'Vacancy' sign out," the little old woman said peevishly.

"I just forgot to take it in, ma'am. Sorry."

"Don't look like you're full," the man complained. "There ain't but one car back there. I looked as we drove up."

I could feel my nerves unraveling. "Mister," I said tightly, "I've got no vacancy. Why don't you try one of the other motels? There are plenty of them down the road."

"The good places are all filled," the old woman whined.

The man said, "Look here, son, I'm not as young as I used to be. Driving tires me, and I've been driving all day. You sure you haven't got some kind of place?"

"For Christ's sake!" I exploded. "How many times do I have to tell you? We've got no vacancy!"

"Well!" The little old woman pulled herself up, outraged. The fat man got red in the face. I turned my back on them and went back to the station as they drove off.

I was still shaking. I took the "Vacancy" sign down and put the "No Vacancy" up, the first time it had been up since I started running the place.

At that moment Paula stepped through the station doorway. She had washed her face and combed her hair and put on fresh lipstick and she looked like ten million dollars.

"Have you called your father?" she said.

"I'm not dragging my father into this, Paula. That's something you'd better get straight."

Surprisingly, she smiled. "All right. If that's the way you want it." She stood up, lazily, like a young savage. Then she stepped to the wall phone and picked up the thin directory.

"What are you doing?"

"I'm going to call a doctor, any doctor."

"You can't! Any doctor you call will have to report that gunshot wound!"

"It can't be helped," she said, as though it didn't make any difference to her one way or the other. "Karl will die if that arm doesn't get attention."

"Then let him die!" I took Paula's arms and held her tight. "What do you care what happens to him? You don't love him. You despise him. I can see it in your eyes every time you look at him."

I must have been hurting her, but she only shrugged. "Maybe, Joe," she said softly, "but he's been good to me."

"What's that supposed to mean?"

This time her smile was edged with bitterness. "Joe," she said huskily, "could you guess what I was before Karl married me? Could you guess what I did for a living?"

I turned her loose. I could guess.

"That's the reason I won't let him die," she said. "Love has nothing to do with it. Karl has everything to gain and nothing to lose by calling a doctor. If the wound is reported, if the story gets to the police—well, it was you that killed the watchman, Joe." She found a number, then lifted the receiver, and I could hear the operator answer.

I slammed the hook down with my hand.

"Well, Joe?" she asked softly.

She had me and she knew it. I picked up the phone and gave the number.

"Hello, Dad?"

## Chapter Eleven

It was closing time but I was still at the station, waiting, wondering what I was going to say when my father came out of that cabin, wondering how I was going to explain it to him. Then I heard his footsteps—those slow, weary footsteps—as he came around to the front of the station. He looked a hundred years old as he came in and set down his bag.

"How's the patient, Dad?" It sounded insane, but he didn't seem to notice.

"Blood poisoning," he said heavily. "Another day without attention would have killed him. He still stands a chance of losing that arm." He reached for the phone and I jumped.

"Who're you calling, Dad?"

"The Sheriffs office. That man has a gunshot wound and I have to report it."

"But it was an accident, Dad. Didn't they tell you?" I was hoping that he wouldn't notice how I was sweating. "You don't have to report it, do you, if it was an accident?"

"All gunshot wounds have to be reported and investigated, Joe. You know that." He reached for the phone again and I stopped his hand with mine.

"Dad, as a favor to me, don't report this one. These people are friends of mine and I know it will be all right. Just don't bother them."

Those old eyes looked puzzled, and I couldn't tell whether he suspected anything or not. "Joe," he said slowly, "you know I have to make a report. I'd be breaking the law if I didn't."

"Then you'll have to break the law, Dad." And that was when he began to notice things. He noticed the sweat, the veins standing out on my forehead, and I guess he saw some things in my eyes that scared him. He felt for a chair and sat down very slowly.

"What is it you're trying to tell me, Joe?"

I couldn't tell him. I couldn't bring myself to hurt him any more than was absolutely necessary, but he knew something was wrong, and he knew it was bad. And he was waiting.

"Joe," he said finally, "you're in trouble, aren't you?"

"Yes."

"Is it bad?"

I couldn't look at him. I nodded.

He just sat there, looking at his hands. Those white, thin hands. After a moment he said quietly, "Why did you do it, Joe? Was it because of that woman?"

I didn't understand at first. Then it began to come, and an unexpected hope began growing inside me. He thought *I* had shot Sheldon! I took hold of that hope and held it tight, I held it with all the strength that was in me.

And then I was talking. "Dad, I don't know how it happened. I'd tell you if I could, but I don't know." I saw the opening and the words came pouring out. "You saw what kind of woman she is. When she came playing around, I lost my head, I guess. I know that's not much of an excuse, but that's the way it was. And lien her husband found out what was going on, and there was a scuffle. I don't know.... There was a gun in it somewhere, and it went off, and when it was over there was a bullet in his arm."

He just sat there.

"Dad," I said, "don't you see why you can't turn in that report? The whole story would come out and the whole town would know about it."

He folded and unfolded those white hands, saying nothing.

"Dad, the rest of my life depends on what you do about this report Should one mistake be that expensive? Just one mistake!"

"I was thinking about Beth," he said heavily. "I didn't want to meddle any more in your affairs, Joe, but that woman, that man's wife, is she the one? Is she the reason you and Beth stopped seeing each other?"

I said nothing and let him think what he wanted to think. His hands trembled as he fumbled for his handkerchief and wiped aimlessly at his forehead.

I couldn't tell how I was doing. I couldn't tell what he was thinking or how much of the story he believed. "Dad," I said tightly, "you hold the lives of three people in your hands. What happens to us now is up to you."

He was hurt, but not nearly as hurt as he would have been

if I had told him the truth. He looked at me once, then picked up his bag and slowly got to his feet. "Fm tired, Joe, very tired. I think I'll go home now."

"The report, Dad. What are you going to do about it?"

He smiled then, and it was the saddest expression I'd ever seen. "It's a terrible thing," he said, "holding other people's lives in your, hands. It makes an old man out of you. Maybe you were right, Joe, in not wanting to be a doctor."

"The report?"

"I've never broken the law, that I know of." And he smiled that sad smile again. "Maybe I'm overdue." He walked out of the station, a little older, a little more bent, a little more tired. Relief washed over me like an icy sea. "I'll come back tomorrow," he said wearily, "and treat the man's arm."

"Tomorrow night, Dad, after I've closed the station. It has to be at night."

"All right. Tomorrow night." He got into his car, a battered old Dodge, and I stood there in the station doorway as he drove onto the highway and headed toward town. I felt as though the weight of the universe had been lifted from my shoulders. I took great gulps of air into my lungs and felt young again, and strong.

I never closed the station faster than I did that night. I took in the hose and oil displays, I locked the pumps and the door, and when I headed for Number 2 it was all I could do to keep from running.

Paula had the door open for me. "What happened?"

"It's all right," I said. I walked over to the bed where Sheldon lay quietly, his eyes closed. "How about him?"

"He's asleep. What did you tell your father?"

"I told you everything was all right. He thinks *I* shot your husband."

She blinked. That was all. Then she laughed. "Your father didn't like me Very much. He didn't approve of me. He thinks I led you astray, doesn't he?"

"Something like that."

"And he knows about the robbery?"

"Not a thing. He doesn't even suspect anything."

"Well," she said, smiling, "you've got brains. I'm glad you didn't disappoint me by not using them."

There never was another woman like Paula Sheldon. She didn't have to talk. What she had to say she could say with her eyes and her body. I lit a cigarette for her and one for me, and we stood there for one long moment saying nothing. Suddenly I reached for her, but she stepped aside as gracefully as a cat.

"No!"

"What's the matter with you?"

"I think you'd better go to your cabin," she said. "You look like you could use some sleep." Carelessly she dropped her cigarette to the floor and stepped on it, then she went over to the bed and placed the back of her hand to Sheldon's forehead. I followed and put one arm around her.

"That's enough," she said flatly.

I wheeled her around, pinning her arms to her side, and when I put my mouth to hers it was like setting fire to a keg of powder. Her arms went around my neck. She melted and flowed against me and I could feel the nervous ripple of her body, the softness of her, the heat of her.

Then it was over. She slipped away.

"You'd better go."

"Like hell!" I reached for her again and she whipped her hand across my face with a crack like a pistol shot in the silence of the room.

"Get out of here!" she hissed.

I almost hit her. I could feel the muscles in my shoulders and arms grow taut as I took a quick step toward her. She didn't move. She just stood there smiling that insolent smile, and I grabbed her by the front of her dress and slammed her against the wall. She went reeling back, then fell over a chair and went down to her hands and knees. Even then, in the midst of rage, I thought what a hell of a woman she was. I had to force myself to turn and walk out. If she had said one word, I would have come running. But she made no sound.

I took a shower and felt a little better. I opened all the doors and windows of my cabin to let in what little breeze there was. I lay across the bed in my shorts and tried to think about my life before Paula came into it, but the picture wouldn't come. It was hard to believe that I had ever been such a person.

Relax, I told myself. Relax and get some sleep.

Easier said than done. Paula had played hell with me. I

could feel myself winding up tighter and tighter, and pretty soon I'd be ready to get up and start kicking holes in the wall.

That was when I heard it. A quick, soft shuffling outside. Then my door opened and Paula was standing there in the doorway, framed in moonlight, as pale as the moon herself. I sat up in bed as she came toward me.

She didn't say a word. She slipped onto the bed and her fingers were like a hundred snakes crawling over my body. "Goddamn you," I said, "I ought to beat your brains out!"

She laughed softly. That hot mouth found me in the darkness and I pulled her down with me.

"Joe?"

"Yes?"

"What were you thinking about before I came?"

"Nothing."

She laughed again.

# Chapter Twelve

It was about two the next afternoon when Ike Abrams came back with the news. His drowsy eyes were bright with the excitement. "By God,", he said, "Creston's about to bust loose at the seams! They just found old Otto Finney's body in the lake!"

"They what!"

"The old watchman at the box factory. They just found his body."

I couldn't believe it. Otto Finney was at the bottom of the lake, where I had dumped him. He had to be!

"A funny thing," Ike said, "the way it happened. You know that upper part of the lake has always been bothered with garfish and big cats. Well, the city opened that part of the lake to commercial fishermen, hoping they'd clean out the scavengers before they ruined it for game fish. Well, this morning these fishermen brought up something that damn near tore their nets to pieces, and it turned out to be a body. It was pretty much of a mess, I guess. All they had to go by for identification was his clothes."

"Is it a positive identification?"

"According to the Sheriff, it is. And you know what kept old Otto underwater all this time? They had him wired to a flywheel."

I couldn't think of a thing to say. I was stunned.

"They say Otis Miller is fit to kill about it. I sure wouldn't want to be in the killer's shoes, with the Sheriff in that frame of mind."

"Does he have anything to go on, any clues?" Ike shrugged. "You know the Sheriff. He doesn't say a thing until he's ready to slip the noose around somebody's neck." Then he noticed the blue Buick in the carport next to Number 2. "I see our star boarders are still with us." He grinned.

That Buick! I should have got rid of it somehow, but it was too late now. I said, "Mr. Sheldon picked up some fever in Texas and doesn't feel like driving. They'll probably be staying over for a day or two."

It didn't sound too good, but Ike took it in stride and was already beginning to sweep the driveway. Then he stopped. "Now that you mention it," he said, "Sheldon didn't look so hot when they came in yesterday. His wife was driving, if I remember right."

I didn't want to talk about the Sheldons; I wanted to hear more about the body. "You say the Sheriff hasn't got any clues to go on?"

"Who knows what Otis Miller has in his mind? All I know is they've got a body and a flywheel. If he could trace the flywheel, it might mean something, but that don't seem very likely. Lot of flywheels around. I think we've got one ourselves in the back of the station."

A coldness was gathering in the pit of my stomach, and I didn't like it. "We had that hauled away the last time the junkman was around," I said quickly.

"Oh?" Ike paused in his sweeping. "I don't remember. The flywheel came out of your dad's old Dodge, though— I remember that much. You don't see them very often these days."

I'd heard enough. I turned the station over Jo Ike and went to my cabin. Then, when the way was clear, I made it over to Number 2. Sheldon was awake but he looked like hell.

"How do you feel?" I asked.

"Lousy." It was barely a whisper.

I went into the kitchen, where Paula was warming some canned soup on the apartment-sized range. She looked at me blankly and it was almost impossible to believe that she was the same woman who had been in my cabin the night before.

"We're in trouble," I said. "They found the body."

She took the pan off the stove. "We had guessed that much, hadn't we?"

"But I hadn't guessed they'd find it this soon. Some commercial fishermen found it this morning, caught that flywheel in their nets."

She didn't seem worried. "It served its purpose. The trail is cold now, just the way you said it would be. They'd never think of looking for the killer in Creston."

"It's the flywheel!" I said. "That goddamn flywheel that we tied the body to. There's just a chance they might trace it back to me. It came out of my dad's old car and I just learned that there aren't many exactly like it."

She thought about it. "That seems pretty farfetched."

"My robbing a payroll and committing murder is pretty farfetched, too, but I did it."

"Has anybody said anything to you, anything at all?"

"No."

She poured the soup into a bowl. "Then stop worrying about it."

"I was just beginning to worry. But I let her take the soup in to Sheldon and watched him sip from the spoon a few times before he fell back to sleep. I took Paula's arm when she came back to the kitchen.

"This is too damn risky," I said, "sitting here right under Otis Miller's nose. You two have got to get out of here, out of Oklahoma."

She smiled wryly. "You weren't so eager to get rid of me last night." She jerked away from me and rinsed the bowl at the kitchen sink. "Besides," she said, "Karl can't be moved."

"He'll have to be moved. My helper at the station is beginning to wonder what the hell is going on back here."

"Let him wonder. He's just a stupid farmer."

"Your husband thought I was a stupid farmer, too, but I cut in for half of that payroll. Get this through your head: We're not as stupid out here as you people seem to think. And we've got a sheriff that's tough, as tough as they come."

She smiled teasingly, and those white arms of hers went around my neck. "You don't really want me to go, do . you, Joe?" She knew the effect she had on a man when she plastered herself against him like that. I grabbed her, holding her tight enough to crush her, but she only smiled.

"Not now, Joe."

"You started it, I didn't!" I forced her head back, and when our mouths came together the contact shocked both of us. Everything went to hell when I touched her. I didn't give a damn about anything or anybody.

I don't know how long we stood there wound up in each other, and I don't know how long Ike had been hollering before I finally heard him.

"Joe! Joe, you in there?"

I almost ignored him. I was tempted to tell him to get away

and leave me alone, because that's the kind of effect Paula Sheldon had on me.

"Joe, the Sheriff wants to talk to you."

That jerked me out of it. It was like having ice water poured on you. Paula hissed, "The Sheriff?" and she couldn't have got away from me faster. "What does he want?"

"I don't know."

"Get out there and see. We can't have him coming in here."

I felt sick. I couldn't imagine what Otis Miller wanted with me, but every bad thing in the world flashed through my mind as I stepped to the door, where Ike was waiting.

"Who did you say wanted me?"

"The Sheriff. He and Ray King are over by your cabin."

Ike was beginning to think things. There were questions behind those sleepy eyes of his that I didn't like at all. Just before I opened the door I thought of something. "Just a minute, Ike." I went back to the kitchen, where Paula was standing like a statue.

"Joe, get out of here!"

I headed straight for the kitchen stove, lifted the grating from one of the cold burners, and smeared my hands good with the collection of burned grease at the bottom. Then I got out.

Ike had already gone back to the station when I came out of Number 2, and the Sheriff and Ray King were standing beside their car, which was parked in front of my own cabin.

"Hello, Sheriff. Hello, Ray. Always something breaking down in a place like this—I just had a kitchen stove to fix for those people." I made sure that they saw the grease on my hands. The Sheriff was sweating, and so was Ray, but I had never felt colder than I was at that moment.

"Just wanted to ask a few questions, Joe," Otis said, "if you can spare us the time."

"Sure, but let's go inside where I can wash up a little." I needed the time to get set for whatever was coming. We went inside and I went into the bathroom and washed my hands. When I came out I felt that I was as ready as I would ever be.

"All right, fellows, what can I do for you?"

Otis sat on the edge of the bed, Ray took a chair, and I stood there in the doorway. "Well," the Sheriff said slowly, "it isn't much, but I can't afford to overlook a thing. You've heard that they found Otto's-body in the lake."

Not trusting my voice, I nodded.

"He was a fine old man," Ray King said softly, and I nodded again, watching the Sheriff. Otis was staring down at his hands, and I couldn't tell what was going on in his mind. Ray King went on: "The picture's pretty clear now, Joe. Old Otto was killed during the robbery and his fingerprints were planted all over the place to throw us off the trail. The whole town's worked up about it. So is the Sheriff, and so am I. We want that killer, Joe, we want him bad!"

"I know how you feel," I said. "I liked Otto, too. I guess everybody did." My voice sounded all right. It was calm enough.

The Sheriff raised his head. "The point Ray's trying to make, Joe, is that we can't overlook a thing, no matter how small, if there is a chance in a million it might help us. That's the reason we're here."

"I understand, Otis."

"Well, here it is. The day before the robbery you were out to the box factory, weren't you?"

So that was it. "That's right," I said. "I stopped by to pay Pat Sully some money I owed him."

"So Pat told me. Joe, were you going somewhere else and just happened to drop by, or did you make a special trip just to see Pat?"

"Why, I guess I made the trip special. I was downtown and just happened to think of it—that's the way I do things sometimes." I didn't like the way this was going. I couldn't tell where it was leading or what they were thinking. They just sat there dead-faced, their eyes expressionless.

"Now tell me this, Joe. Did you notice anything out of the way while you were out there that day?"

I could hear my heart pounding. "What do you mean, Sheriff?"

"I mean you used to work at the box factory and were pretty familiar with the place. You knew all the people, the buildings. It occurred to me that a person who hadn't been out there for a while might notice something that people who work there every day might pass by. I just want to know if you noticed anything out of the way, no matter how small—something that might help us."

I made a show of thinking it over. "I'm sorry, Sheriff, I can't think of a thing."

"Tell me just what you did while you were out there."

"Did? Well, not much. I just went in and gave Pat the money I owed him and left. I wasn't there more than two or three minutes."

"I see." Otis took off his Stetson and wiped the sweat-band with his handkerchief. "Well, it was just a chance. I've talked to everybody at the factory, and they're not much help. There's one more thing, Joe, if you don't mind."

"Sure."

"It's out there in the car. I want you to take a look at something."

What was he getting at now? Was it a trick? Was he beginning to suspect something or was it just routine? I felt as though my nerve ends had worked to the top of my skin. If anybody had touched me I'd have yelled.

But I managed to keep a straight face as we filed out of the cabin. Ike Abrams was standing at the corner of the station, watching us, and Otis called to him. "Come on back here, Ike, if you're not busy." And then he opened the car door and there it was, on the floor.

The flywheel that I had tied to the body.

"Have you ever seen this before, Joe?"

At that moment I was completely defeated, crushed. My tongue was thick and my throat tight, and I knew I couldn't utter a word if my life depended on it. To gain time, I pushed my head and shoulders into the back of the car and pretended to take a close look at the flywheel. My God, I thought, he knows everything! He must! Why else would he bring that thing straight to me?

It was a bad moment. But it passed. I made my hands stop trembling. By sheer force of will I made myself stand up and say calmly, "Is this the flywheel that was tied to the body?"

"That's right. Did you ever see it before?"

"I don't think so. Of course, I can't be sure. Ike works on cars sometimes, back of the station, and leaves extra parts around."

"What do you do with those extra parts?"

"Have them hauled away with the tin cans and other trash

that piles up in a place like this. Maybe once a month I call a truck and have the stuff taken out to the dumping grounds."

"I see." Then he said, "Ike, how about you? You ever see a flywheel like this before?"

"Sure," Ike said, and my insides seemed to shrivel.

"Have you ever seen *this* one before?"

"Can't be sure about that. But it looks like one that used to be back in the station."

"What makes you say that?"

"Well..." Ike pushed closer and had a good look. "Well, the ring gear is still on it, for one thing. See how chewed up it is? It looks like the assembly I took out of Dr. Hooper's old Dodge not too long ago. He had a bad habit of pushing the starter while the engine was running— absent-minded, I guess—and that's the reason the ring gear is chewed up the way it is. Had a hell of a time with the pinion gear jamming."

"Is that the reason you replaced the flywheel?"

"Hell, no. Just a new ring gear would have fixed that part of it. That old car of his had a bad clutch that scored a flywheel. Had to replace the whole assembly."

"When was that?"

"Maybe a month ago. A little longer."

Otis turned to me. "Have you had the trash hauled since then?"

That was the big question. That was the jackpot question, and it could kill me if I didn't come up with the right answer.

That clutch, that flywheel, they had been taken out together, and it was reasonable to assume that they had been hauled away together. If they had been hauled away. If both of them were still in the station, everything would be fine. But I knew they weren't. If both of them were gone, that would be fine, too. But that clutch was still there.

You'd better think fast, Hooper.

And I couldn't think at all. I stood there with my forehead screwed up, trying to look as if I was thinking, but there was just a roaring emptiness in my brain. There was only one thing to do. I had to bluff it. I had to lower my head and bull my way through, and hope that Otis Miller would take it.

I heard myself saying, "Sure, all that stuff was hauled away almost a month ago. It's about time I called the truck again."

"Ike would remember the hauling, wouldn't he?"

That was the end. I might as well get set for it. I looked at Ike and knew that he would be no help at all. "Sure," I said, surprised to hear that my voice was still normal. "I guess Ike would remember."

Ike was scratching his head, looking a bit sheepish. "Sheriff," he said slowly, "I can't be sure when the last hauling was done, but I think I know what you're getting at. You're trying to trace that flywheel, is that right?"

"It's the only clue we have. That's right, Ike."

"The flywheel I mentioned we had in the station, do you figure it's the same one you have in your car?"

The Sheriff said nothing. He just waited.

"Well," Ike went on, "like I said, I don't remember exactly about the hauling. But I do remember that clutch assembly, because I took it home with me."

The Sheriff's eyes widened. He looked as though he had reached for his gun and discovered it wasn't there. "What do you mean, Ike—you took it home with you?"

"Well..." Ike was sweating now. He knew that he had just kicked one of Otis Miller's ideas full of holes. I felt like the man who got a reprieve after they had already strapped him to the chair. I could hear relief whistling through my teeth. Suddenly I could smile. I could breathe again. Riding this kind of luck, nothing could stop me. Nothing! It was all I could do to keep from laughing.

The Sheriff was waiting.

"Well," Ike said again, "I figured Joe wouldn't mind. I had an idea I could use some of the parts sometime."

"Have you still got that clutch assembly?"

"Sure. At home." Then Ike got smart, as he sometimes did. He stopped talking.

The Sheriff looked at Ike, then at me, then he took off his hat and wiped his face. Then, surprisingly, he grinned. "Well, I guess that's all. Sorry to have bothered you, Joe."

"Not at all, Sheriff." He could never in the world pin anything on me now, no matter what he was thinking behind that grin.

Then Otis turned to Ray King. "We'd better be going. I want to check with all garages and salvage yards on this thing."

Ike and I stood there as they got into the car and drove out to the highway. My feeling of elation began to melt as the car disappeared. It had been a close thing—too close for comfort. If Otis had caught me in that lie about the flywheel, it would have been all over.

# Chapter Thirteen

I used the stove-repair excuse on Ike again and back to the Sheldon cabin. Paula had the question ready before I got the door open.

"What did the Sheriff want?"

"I don't know what he wanted. He was very polite, but that doesn't mean a thing with Otis Miller."

"What kind of questions did he ask?"

"It isn't the questions that matters. Most of them didn't make sense. But he had that damn flywheel with him. That's the important thing."

Sheldon was awake again. He had been following the talk with his eyes closed, but now he opened them. His voice was husky, not much more than a whisper.

"He didn't trace the flywheel to you, did he?"

"Not for sure, but he may have ideas. There's no way of telling about a man like Otis." I went over to the bed and said, "How do you feel?"

"Like hell."

"You'd better take a turn for the better, because you've got to get out of here."

Paula stepped between us.

"Look," I said tightly, "I know what I'm talking about. This sheriffs no dummy. Sooner or later he'll begin tying all the loose ends together, and that will be the end of us."

"We'll leave," Paula said calmly, "when the doctor says it's all right. Not before."

I could feel anger swelling in my throat. Tread lightly, I told myself. Take it easy and think straight. I turned and walked out.

Paula followed me out of the cabin and caught me at the bottom step. "This is the way it has to be, Joe. I don't like it any better than you do, but I can't leave him to die." She looked at me. Then she took my hand and I could feel the current going up my arm. "It's going to work out all right, Joe."

"You don't know the Sheriff."

"It's going to work out. I can feel it. Karl will be ready to travel before long. When things cool off, you can contact me through my sister, just the way we planned."

I wanted her, but I also wanted to stay alive. I said "That husband of yours is going to get us nothing but trouble. Leave him to me and I'll get rid of our troubles before they kill us."

Her eyes snapped angrily. "No! Can't I make you understand? I owe Karl something, I owe him plenty, and this is the only way I can pay him back. Seeing him through this is the only way I'd ever feel right about leaving him."

"This is a hell of a time to develop scruples about paying your debts!"

"Nevertheless, that's the way it is. I'm no good, Joe, but neither am I completely rotten."

"All right!" I was mad, but not so mad that I didn't realize that I had to get away from there. "Nurse him back to health, if you can. Take your time. Everything's going to be just dandy." I went back to the station and worked on the grease rack until I had calmed down.

It was a long day. They don't come any longer than that one.

I couldn't keep my mind on business for wondering about the Sheriff and whether or not he actually suspected anything. I knew one thing—I had to get hold of my father and have him patch Sheldon up well enough to travel. Every minute they remained in Creston piled more odds on Otis Miller's side of this thing.

I called my dad twice that afternoon but he wasn't home. There was nothing to do but wait.

I was on edge again when Ike came in, wearing that stupid grin of his.

"Well," I said, "maybe you'll tell me what's so goddamn funny."

Ike didn't bat an eye. "You know," he said, "you're beginnin' to act just like Frank Sewell when he broke up with his wife. Damn if he wasn't the hardest man to live with you ever saw."

"If I'm so hard to live with," I said, "maybe you'd like to gather up your work clothes and quit."

"Nope," Ike said quietly. "I figure you'll get over it after a while."

I never figured that Ike fancied himself as any cupid, but I could see that he was trying to swing the conversation around to me and Beth Langford. That was about the next to the last thing in the world I wanted to talk about.

I had to get away. I went around to the wash rack and cleaned the place up a little, and pretty soon I began to cool off. After a while I went back to Ike and apologized for blowing up. I had to stay on the good side of him. I wanted him to go on thinking that everything was exactly the way it always had been.

Around six o'clock I told Ike that I'd close the station myself and sent him home.

It was well after dark when my dad came back to have another look at the patient. He was a very old man that night as he got out of his car and said heavily, "You all right, Joe?"

"Sure, Dad, I'm fine. I want to talk to you when you finish back there."

He took off his hat and ran his fingers through his thinning hair. All the things my son could have been! I could see him thinking it. I could see it in those ancient, melancholy eyes. Then he nodded. "All right, Joe." And he walked heavily back to Number 2.

That was when the black Ford rolled up in front of the station. I went out automatically and reached for the gas hose. The car door opened and a man said, "Never mind, Hooper."

I froze.

He was a big man with a big, humorless grin. He wore a straw sombrero and a loud sport shirt. His name was Bunt Manley.

## Chapter Fourteen

He didn't get out of the car. He sat there for a moment, grinning. Then he started the car and drove around to the side of the station and parked. When he came back I was still standing there, frozen, feeling the bottom falling out of everything.

"Wasn't that your dad headed back toward the cabins, Hooper?"

There were no words in me at that moment.

"Sure it was your dad," Manley said. "Could it be there's somebody back there needs a doctor? You know, that's a right interesting idea. I think I'll just go back and give the doc a hand."

"Stay where you are," I said. "My father doesn't like to be bothered when he's caring for a patient."

"I'll bet," he said dryly. "Especially if the patient happens to be a man named Karl Sheldon."

That was it. I didn't know how he knew, but he did. He knew everything. He stood there looking at me, half grinning, then he fished out a cigarette and lighted it. "You know," he said roughly, "you're really quite a boy, Hooper. Tell you the truth, I didn't think you had the guts for a thing like this."

I had to bluff it, there was no other way. "I don't know what you're talking about, Bunt."

He laughed suddenly. "You know damn well what I'm talking about." Then, surprisingly, he turned on his heel and went to his car. But he was back almost immediately, with a newspaper in his hand. "Here," he said. "I want to read you a little piece of news that turned up in yesterday's paper. Date-lined Crowell, Texas. 'Last night Frank Hennessy, city marshal of Crowell, Texas, prevented the burglary of a city drugstore...' So on and so on, but here's the interesting part. 'Hennessy was able to provide descriptions of the would-be burglars. The man was of tall, athletic build. He had dark, thick hair, and was well dressed. In all probability the man is carrying one of the Marshal's bullets in his body. The man's woman companion was slight of build with short blonde hair."

Looking at me, Manley folded the paper. "You heard enough, Hooper?"

"I still don't know what you're talking about."

He wasn't grinning now. "I'm talking about that blue Buick back there in one of your carports, Hooper. I saw it this afternoon and began putting two and two together." He snapped his cigarette straight at my feet. "Funny thing about it, though. I never tied you in with them until just now, when I saw your old man headed back to that shack. Sheldon's been here two days, hasn't he? And your old man has been taking care of him. Now, does it stand to reason that Doc Hooper would treat a bullet wound and not report it—unless he had a mighty good reason?" He reached out quickly and grabbed the front of my shirt. "I know the reason, Hooper. He's doing it to keep his son out of the electric chair!"

Something snapped when I felt those thick fingers grab me. A rage caught fire inside me and I wasn't afraid any more, I was just mad. I knocked his hand away and then grabbed his arm and slammed him against the station wall. "Listen," I said hoarsely. "Listen to me, you sonofabitch. If you try to drag my father into this thing, I'll kill you!"

He was startled. He hadn't expected this kind of reaction. "Look here!"

"You look, Manley! And don't you forget! So help me God, I'll kill you if my father is brought into this!" I let him go and he almost fell.

I had learned one thing these past few days. You had to be tough if you didn't want people stepping on you. You had to let them know who was boss, even if you had to beat it into their thick skulls.

"All right," I said, still shaking with rage. "You think you know something. You think you've got me nailed, don't you?"

"Wait a minute, Hooper! For Christ's sake!"

And only then did I realize that I was about to hit him. My fist was a hard club, ready to smash into that thick face of his. I think I would have killed him at that moment, right on the spot, if I hadn't suddenly snapped out of it. And Manley knew it. Maybe, at that moment, Bunt Manley was remembering that old watchman that they had fished out of the lake.

When I relaxed he began to breathe again, but not very well. "For Christ's sake, Hooper, I haven't got anything against you! It's them!"

"Who's them?"

"You know who I mean. Karl Sheldon and that wife of his. I've got something coming from them, but not from you, Hooper."

"What have you got coming from Sheldon and his wife?"

"Well, it was my idea, wasn't it? That box factory?" He was thinking a little faster now. "After all, I was the one that got in touch with Sheldon and told him about it. He was supposed to cut me in on it. I want my share of the money, that's all."

"You're not getting a penny, Manley. And you're not going to mention my father. Is that clear?"

"Sure, Hooper, I told you it wasn't *you* I was after. And what could I gain by bringing your old man in on a thing like this?"

"I just wanted to be sure you had it straight."

I was thinking. Maybe—just maybe—Bunt Manley had a point here. It was a lousy piece of luck that he had to know at all, but he did, and there was nothing I could do to change that. If he could somehow talk Sheldon out of part of his take, maybe it would be a good idea. Maybe that would satisfy him and he would be quiet.

But I knew, even then, that it was wishful thinking. Manley would never be satisfied. There was too much greed in those quick little eyes. And besides, Paula would never turn loose a penny of that money; I had seen enough of her to know that.

The answer was clear, and I think Manley was beginning to get it now. I went around to his car and took his keys, just in case he decided this wasn't such a good place to butt in, after all.

"What are you doing?" he asked quickly.

"Nothing. I think we ought to talk this over with Sheldon and his wife, that's all. After my father gets out of there."

I had a tire tool in my hand, a nice, solid piece of iron, and Manley knew I would use it if he made a move. He didn't make the move. After a while I heard those dragging steps again and my dad came around the side of the station. I took hold of Manley's arm and squeezed it hard. "Just remember," I said. "Dad, is that you?"

"Yes, Joe."

I went around to the side of the station where he was standing, as though he didn't want to look at me in the light. "Is he all right, Dad?"

"Yes, he's better, Joe."

"Is he able to travel, Dad? They want to go as soon as possible."

"Yes," he said, "he'll be able to travel tomorrow." I had almost forgotten how stooped and small he was. He said quietly, without looking at me, "Is that all, Joe?"

"Yes, Dad, I guess that's all. And thanks for everything."

He made no answer. He stood there for a moment, his head bowed, and then he turned and walked slowly to his car.

I stood there, feeling lousy about the way I had hurt him. Then I thought: Just be glad he doesn't know the real truth. That's the one thing in this mess you can be glad of.

I turned to Manley, the tire tool still in my hand. He must have been a mindreader, that Manley. He stared at me for maybe five seconds and knew all the answers. He could look into his future and see nothing but the endless darkness of death.

"Joe, for Christ's sake!"

"Just shut up," I said, "until I get this station locked up." And that was when he started to run. He knew now that he had made a mistake—a lot of mistakes. In the first place, he should have brought a gun with him if he figured on taking a slice of that thirty thousand dollars. But the small detail of a gun had slipped his mind, and now there was no way out except to run for it.

He moved fast. It's hard to believe that a man his size could move as fast as he did—but it wasn't fast enough for the tire tool. I drew back and let it fly, and it caught him right in the middle of the back, about three inches below the shoulders. He dropped as though he had been shot.

I thought he was dead at first. I turned him over with my foot and his eyes had that glazed look that I had seen before. But his pulse was still there, and he was still breathing. I rolled him over to the wash rack and locked up the station.

I had no feeling at all for Manley. The lousy chisler had tried to horn in on money that I had risked my life for, and he deserved to be dead. But I was glad he wasn't, just yet. This time somebody else was going to pull the trigger. This time somebody else was going to have the pressure put on him, not me.

I was thinking fast now. There was one thing I knew —Paula Sheldon was the one woman in the world for me. That I was sure of. But how could I be sure that I was the man for her? What if she turned against me sometime in the future? She was the one person who could get me electrocuted, because she knew that it was my gun that had killed Otto Finney.

Think this out carefully, Hooper. You need Paula Sheldon the way an alcoholic needs his booze. But what if she decided to leave you? There's nothing you can do about it, because she's holding a knife at your throat.

What I needed was a knife like hers, and I thought I knew just how to get it.

There was very little traffic on the highway, and for once in my life I was glad that there were no customers. After I got the station locked up, I went around to the wash rack and saw that Manley was just beginning to come out of it. I pulled him up by one arm and half dragged him back to the Sheldons' cabin.

Paula's pale face got even paler when I came in with Manley. Even Sheldon showed signs of life.

"Hooper, what the hell..."

I dumped Manley right in the middle of the floor and looked at both of them. "So you had to come back to Creston," I said tightly. "I told you this thing was going to blow up right in our faces if you didn't get out of here."

Paula was standing very erect, as cold and pale as marble. "How much does Manley know?"

I had the feeling that she was scared, actually scared for the first time. It was good to know that I wasn't the only person in this thing with some feelings. "He knows everything," I said. "Every damn thing there is to be known."

"How?" Sheldon asked.

"Because of that stupid drugstore job of yours in Texas. It was in the paper and Manley saw it. Then, out of curiosity, probably, he drove out this way and saw that Buick of yours. Not even Manley is so stupid that he couldn't fill in the rest for himself."

"What does he want?" Sheldon said weakly. "A share of the money?"

"That's what he said. But I've got an idea he won't be satisfied for anything less than the whole take."

Sheldon looked even sicker than before. He'd had enough. There was nothing in the world he would like better than to undo everything that had happened and forget that he had ever heard of Creston, Oklahoma. At that moment I think Sheldon would gladly have given up every penny.

But not Paula. She had recovered from the first shock of seeing me drag Manley into the place, and now that gleaming, steel-trap brain of hers was working as coolly as ever. She turned her gaze on Manley, who was trying to lift himself to his hands and knees without much success. Shaking his head dumbly, he moved as though the right side of his body were paralyzed, and maybe it was.

Still looking at Manley, Paula spoke to me. "You shouldn't have brought him here. You should have killed him."

"I've had my share of killing."

Her head snapped up. "You've gone yellow?"

"If you want to call it that. It's just that I don't intend to carry more than my load in this thing. You brought this on when you came back here. You can get out of it the best way you can."

Surprisingly, she smiled. "I think I called you a stupid farmer once. I apologize."

There was absolutely no way of knowing what she would do or how she would react. She showed admiration only when I lashed out the hardest.

"What are we going to do?" Sheldon asked hoarsely from the bed.

"That's up to you. Or your wife." I looked at both of them and knew that it was going to have to be Paula. Not until then did I realize that I was still carrying that tire tool in my hand—but Paula had noticed. She took it from me.

Manley never knew what hit him. Still dazed, he was trying to bring himself to his knees when Paula swung. It was the first time I had ever heard the mushy sound of a skull caving in. It's a sound I won't soon forget. Manley fell on his face, kicked once, and then was completely still. There was very little blood.

Everything in the room seemed to freeze for just a moment.

I hadn't been ready for anything as cold-blooded as this, and neither had Sheldon. He lifted himself up in bed for just an instant, staring wide-eyed at Manley, who was dead. There was no doubt about that; he was dead. Then Sheldon made a thin little sound, almost a kittenish sound, and dropped back on the pillow.

Only Paula took it completely in stride. She looked at the tire tool, then wiped it neatly on Manley's shirt and put it to one side. She said, "He came in a car, didn't he?"

I nodded.

"Get it. Bring it back here." Her breathing came slightly faster than usual, it was the only way her excitement betrayed her. She stood very straight and brushed her hair away from her forehead. "Mr. Manley," she said, "is going to have a very bad accident."

An "accident" was the only way. My father had seen Bunt Manley with me just a few minutes before; that fact immediately canceled out any attempt to get rid of the body. Sure as hell the Sheriff would be back asking more questions, and that was the last thing in the world I could allow to happen. I said, "All right. I'll get his car."

## Chapter Fifteen

I knew just where it had to happen, and how. I looked at my watch and it was almost eleven o'clock—just about time enough if we worked fast. I carried Manley's body out to his car and dumped him into the front seat. Paula stayed behind long enough to clean up what little blood there was on the floor, and then she came out and said, "I'll follow you in the Buick."

"All right. We don't have far to go." My heart was beating like a hammer against my rib cage.

"This part is up to you," she said. "Do you know exactly what you're going to do?"

"Exactly. Now get in that Buick and follow me. Turn your headlights off when you see mine go out."

She touched my arm. "You're all right, Joe," she said huskily. "You're a lot of man."

"Thanks," I said flatly.

"I wanted you to know, Joe."

"You told me. Now get in the Buick."

She got into the Buick and I got into Manley's car. The body was sprawled all over the floor boards and I had to shove it over in order to get my foot on the brake pedal. I turned on the switch and started the motor.

When I got to the highway I slowed down until the Buick's headlights showed in my rear-view mirror. I looked at my watch again and it was ten minutes after eleven—still enough time. I hit thirty-five on the speedometer and held it there. Take it slow and easy. This is the one time in your life when you can't afford to pick up a highway patrolman, Hooper.

About two miles outside of Creston, just on the other side of the oil-field supply houses, I turned off the highway and eased down to a crawl until I was sure that Paula was still behind me. We followed the graveled road for maybe a mile, until I could see a stand of tall cottonwoods in the headlights. That was the thing I was looking for. Just beyond the cottonwoods I saw the outstretched arms of a railroad-crossing sign and I snapped off my lights. The Buick's lights went out behind me and both of us slowed down to a crawl again. Just before reaching the crossing I stopped the car.

Eleven-twenty, my watch said. It was time. I got out of the car and the country road was completely deserted. Paula, in the Buick, was about fifty yards back, pulled off on the gravel shoulder. I knew that she must have figured it out by now, because she made no move to get— out of the car.

I walked up the slight grade to the crossing and listened until my ears hurt, but there were only the million little sounds that come with the night. I got down on my knees and put an ear to the rail, but I couldn't be sure whether I heard anything or not. My watch said eleven-twenty-five.

The Rock Island Rocket, unless they had changed schedule, hit Creston at eleven-fifteen on the dot, stopping just long enough to take on express. From this crossing to Creston, as well as I could judge, was about eight miles. It shouldn't take a train like the Rocket more than ten minutes to cover eight miles.

Then I heard it. The rasping sound of its horn cut the night like a knife. I hurried back to the car and got it started. I slammed it forward until it exactly straddled the tracks, and then I saw the light. The dazzling brilliance of that single enormous headlight sprang up like a thousand suns on the other side of the cottonwoods. I thought, I've got to get out of here, and fast! I kicked the door open. All I could think of was getting out of there. Then I caught my arm on something, my wrist. I didn't know what was holding me and I was too excited „to find out. That locomotive was crashing around that stand of cottonwoods, the noise filling the night, and then I gave my arm a hard tug and it was free. I ran.

I never ran faster.

Paula had the Buick running by the time I got there. She had the door open and I dived in.

"Is everything all right?"

"Yes."

"Joe, are you sure?"

"Goddamnit, I said yes!"

Then she slammed the car in gear, and we had traveled maybe fifty feet when all hell broke loose behind us. Fire lit up the sky like worlds colliding, and the locomotive slammed into Manley's car. The engineer didn't have a chance to stop, he didn't see the car until he was on top of it. I heard the nerve-shattering screech of steel on steel, and the racket of coupled coaches slamming together, and then the locomotive crashed headlong into the car, scattering it all over the countryside. I looked back once and that was enough.

Paula and I rode in tense silence until we hit the highway. Then she said, "Joe..." and I stared straight ahead. "Joe, are you sorry?"

"About Manley? It's a little late to be sorry, isn't it?"

She smiled. At a time like that she could smile. After a moment she said quietly, "You're quite a man, Joe, you really are. You're hard and you're tough. You're a lot tougher than you think."

I said nothing. I was still hearing that locomotive slamming into Manley's car.

She leaned against me for just a moment. "I mean it, Joe. I've been thinking. I know a place in Arkansas," she said, steering the car through the night, "near Hot Springs. A friend of Karl's lives there. For a price he would take care of Karl for a week or two, however long it takes his arm to get well. Then it will be the two of us, Joe. Just you and me."

I looked at her. "You just now thought of this place?"

"Not exactly," she said softly, almost crooned. "I'll tell you the truth, Joe. Until tonight I wasn't absolutely sure about you."

"Are you sure now?"

"Yes."

And then we were back at the station. Paula drove off the highway and put the car into the port. When she switched off the ignition I reached out for her, brought her hard against me, and pressed her back against the seat, my mouth on hers.

"Yes," she said again, "I'm sure."

She twisted expertly and was out of my arms, but her eyes were glistening with the brightness of excitement. I followed her into the cabin, almost ran over her, for she was standing frozen in the doorway.

"Joe!"

I saw what had stopped her. It was her husband, Karl Sheldon, lying face down on the floor.

I went down on one knee beside him and turned him over. His face was flushed, and the heat of his fever burned my hand as I felt of his forehead. I looked around and saw two suitcases partly packed, and I guessed that, in his eagerness to get away from here, he had tried to pack himself while Paula and I were out disposing of Manley's body. In the middle of the job he must have passed out.

My only emotion was one of anger. Goddamn him, I thought, why didn't he stay in bed? I had a crazy urge to close my fingers around his throat and choke out the little life that was left in him, but instead I lifted him and put him on the bed. Paula felt of his forehead and looked at me.

"Joe, we'll have to get your father."

I tried to hold onto my anger. "Look," I said. "It will just take more time, and time is a thing that could kill us. Not more than an hour ago my father was here. He looked at your husband and said he was able to travel."

"That was an hour ago. He wasn't this sick then. Look at him—does he look in any shape to travel? Do you want him to die?"

"Why not?"

The pressure was being applied and the only thing I could think of was kill. It got to be a fever, a worse fever than the kind Sheldon had. Great God, I thought, what has happened to me in just a few short days? After a moment I took Paula's arm and held it for a moment. "I guess I didn't mean that," I said.

She was in complete control of herself. "You know how I feel about Karl," she said evenly. "I'll leave him, but not now, not like this."

"I said I didn't mean it!" Then I turned for the door and walked out.

There was a night light burning in the station and it felt as bright as those factory floodlights as I lifted the receiver and gave the number. I could hear the ringing. It must have gone on for a full minute before my father answered.

"Dad, can you come out to the station? Right away?"

He didn't say a thing. I could hear his heavy breathing. I could almost feel his weariness. "Dad," I said, "it's important."

"All right, Joe." He hung up. I sat down at the plank desk and tried to tell myself that it was going to be all right. After all, my father didn't know I had anything to do with the robbery and killing. For all he knew, I had just got myself into some kind of fool scrape over a woman. People got into that kind of trouble every day. And Sheriff Miller—if he had anything to throw, he would have hit me with it long before now. Miller meant business. He would have jumped on me good if he'd had any idea I was mixed up in a killing.

He hadn't jumped, so everything was all right. But it didn't feel all right. There was this thing with Manley and my nerves were still raw from that, but I couldn't see how they could possibly tie me up to a train wreck. That part had been foolproof, much better than the lake.

But it didn't feel right. As I sat there I could fed the cold emptiness growing in my guts.

I remembered then how easy it had seemed at first. A pushover robbery, fifteen thousand dollars in my pocket. Easy. What a joke that had been, but I wasn't laughing. Somewhere along the line my future had gone up in a bright, hot flame. It started the day I first looked at Paula Sheldon, and it was sealed the night I eavesdropped at Sheldon's window.

I needed sleep. I got up, went to the far wall of the station, and began moving cases of oil. When I had all the money together I locked the station again and went to my car and stuffed the money under the rear seat. I was just beginning to realize that I was actually preparing to leave Creston, preparing to wipe out in one night the plans that had been half a lifetime in the making. As far back as I could remember I had known just what I wanted—position, respectability, family; the same things, more or less, that every man wants out of life.

And what do you have now, Joe Hooper?

Fifteen thousand dollars. That's a lot of money in any man's language. And Paula Sheldon, if I wanted her on her terms. And I did.

The door to Number 2 opened and Paula said, "Joe, is that you?"

"Yes."

She came outside and over to where I was standing.

"He seems to be sleeping. Did you call your father?"

"He's on his way." She leaned against me and it was like a charge of electricity against my bare arm. I grabbed her, pulled her hard against me, and she squirmed like a snake.

"Joe, not now!"

"What's wrong with now?"

She laughed softly, moving her head to one side as I tried to kiss her. "What were you thinking, Joe, when I called to you just now?"

"Nothing."

She smiled. I felt her hands on my arms, crawling up and down my arms and across my shoulders. Then, deliberately, she gouged her sharp fingernails into the muscles of my shoulders. "You're hard, Joe. I like men who are hard!"

That mouth of hers found mine and everything seemed worth while again. Who gave a damn about the past or the future, as long as there was a present? I held her tight, so tight that I knew I was hurting her, but she made no sound of complaint. My arms and legs felt weak when I finally released her.

"We're getting out of here," I said. "Tonight."

"If your father says it's all right."

"All right or not. It's got to be tonight; I've got to get away from Creston."

She was silent for a moment, then turned her face up to mine. "You really mean it, don't you, Joe? Don't you have any roots here? Don't you feel just a little sorry to leave this place?"

"No."

"What about your father?"

"He'll be better off without me."

"Karl asked you once if you had a girl here in Creston. Do you, Joe?"

"Not any more."

"No girl, no roots."

"Nothing."

"Just me?"

"Just you."

She laughed. The sound of that laughter cut like a whip, and at that moment I could have killed her, and I almost did. I knocked her back against the car and grabbed for her throat. But she was too fast for me. She slipped out of my arms and moved quickly along the side of the car, and there was a flash of uneasiness in her eyes. Not fear, just uneasiness that came from the knowledge that she had done something very dangerous. By the time I got my hands on her again that first unreasoning burst of anger had disappeared, but Paula didn't know it.

"Joe, what's wrong?"

"Nothing's wrong," I said roughly. Then, very gently, I put my hands on her throat and slowly let my fingers begin to squeeze. "Just you, Paula. That's the way you want it, isn't it?"

That was when the first fear showed in her eyes. In my mind were all the things I was giving up for her, and she had laughed at them. I don't know what would have happened if the car hadn't pulled off the highway just then, if the headlights hadn't cut a bright swath across the row of cabins and snapped me out of it. I turned her loose and said, "That must be my father. You'd better go back to Karl."

She slipped away quickly, as silently as the night itself, and I stood there by the car as rigid as steel. Slowly I made myself relax. I told myself that what had happened had been for the best. She knew who was boss now. That was Sheldon's trouble; he had never let her know who was boss.

It didn't occur to me that my father, in his old Dodge, hadn't had time to reach the station. I watched the headlights coming toward me from the highway, and when the car stopped a little way from my cabin I stepped out and said: "Dad, is that you?"

"No, Joe." A thick, squat figure stepped out of the car and said, "It's the Sheriff, Joe. Otis Miller."

## Chapter Sixteen

The muscles in my legs turned to milksop. The Sheriff waited for Ray King to get out of the car and then the two of them came toward me. If my legs could have worked I would have started running in stark panic—but they wouldn't work and that was the only thing that saved me.

Otis Miller said, "Hope we didn't wake you, Joe, comin' out here like this in the middle of the night."

"Not at all, Sheriff." I was amazed that my voice could sound so calm. "Too hot to sleep in that cabin of mine— but we could go in and have a beer. What have you got on your mind?"

"Just some questions, Joe," Ray King said.

At this time of night! But I merely nodded at the door to my cabin and the two of them went in ahead of me. I followed and turned on the light. Otis sat heavily in the room's only armchair and Ray took the edge of the bed. They were very businesslike. Their faces told me nothing.

"How about that beer?" I said. "There's some in the icebox."

Both of them shook their heads. "Later, maybe," Otis said, wiping his face with a handkerchief. "Joe, didn't I see somebody with you as we drove off the highway just a minute ago?"

I was sure they could hear my heart pounding. I had to stand there looking them right in the eye, not knowing what they were thinking, or how much they knew. "Oh, yes," I said, and again my voice sounded all-right. "That was the lady from the next cabin. Her husband came down with the fever. She knew my father was a doctor and wanted me to call him."

"Did you do it?"

"Sure, just before you drove up. He'll be here soon."

I was going to have to explain my father some way when he got here, and I might as well do it now. If Otis and Ray already knew about the Sheldons, there was nothing I could do about it, anyway. I needed a minute to get myself set for whatever was coming, so I said, "Ray, you sure you won't have a beer with me?"

"No, thanks, Joe. Maybe later."

I went into the kitchen and got a can out of the icebox and opened it. Why had they come here at this time of night? Why in heaven's name had they come? I forced myself to calm down. By sheer will power I stuffed my fear down to the bottom of my guts and held it there. Then I went back to them.

"About those questions. Is it anything special, Sheriff?"

"Can't say yet about that Joe, have you been here all night?"

"No, not all night. I closed the station and went into town to see a movie."

"By yourself. No one was with you?"

"No, I was by myself." I tried to grin. "Maybe you've heard; me and Beth Langford kind of called things off."

He hadn't heard and he wasn't interested.

I said, "What's this all about, anyway? Is it so important that it can't wait till morning?"

"It's important enough," Otis said. "Joe, how well did you know Bunt Manley?"

Here it comes, I thought. Buy my voice was a thing apart; it answered calmly. "Bunt Manley? Why, I don't know him very well. He put in some federal time for bootlegging a while back, didn't he?"

"When was the last time you saw Manley?"

I started to say I couldn't remember, but I recalled just in time that my dad had seen me with Manley just a couple of hours ago. It would take too short a memory to forget a thing like that.

I said, "Come to think of it, I saw Bunt Manley tonight. Not more than two hours ago."

"Here at the station?"

"Sure." I felt a little better. I was convinced that I could make up lies as fast as Otis could ask the questions. "Sure," I said again. "He drove up to the station just as I was closing up. He wanted some gas."

"I see. Does Bunt Manley usually trade with you?"

"No, not as a rule. Nearly everybody in town, though, drops in on me at one time or another."

"What did Manley do after he got his gas?"

"Paid me and drove off, that's all. Say, couldn't you give me an idea what this is about?"

"In a minute. When was the last time you saw Manley before tonight?"

I made a show of thinking. "I can't remember, Sheriff. I might have seen him in town, but not to speak to."

"I see. Joe, could you give me the time?"

"Sure." Then I looked at my wrist and my watch wasn't there. "I must have left my watch lying around somewhere," I said, and started toward the dresser. But Otis stopped me.

He held up a watch and said, "Is this yours, Joe?"

That was when the roof fell in. That watch! I didn't know just what part it was going to play in my future, but I knew it wasn't going to be good. I could see it in the Sheriff's eyes, in the tight lines at the corners of Ray King's mouth. There was absolutely no use denying it was my watch. On the back was the legend "Joseph Hooper, Jr. May 16, 1938," engraved in the gold. My dad had given me the watch when I was graduated from high school, and if that engraving wasn't enough to settle it, the local jeweler had the records.

It was my watch, all right. But where had it come from? How had the Sheriff got hold of it? I remembered having it on my wrist only a short time before, because I had been counting the seconds while waiting for that train.

Otis Miller said again, "Is this yours, Joe?"

"Yes, it's mine." That was all I could say.

"Could you guess where we found this watch, Joe?" he asked, his voice silky-smooth, his face bland.

It was like playing barehanded with a swamp moccasin, but I had to play with him until I found out where he was headed. "No, I have no idea where I lost it."

The Sheriff stood up, a rare smile touching the corners of his thick mouth. "You sonofabitch!" he said softly. "You know, all right."

Ray King came out of his chair. "Hold it, Otis. Take it easy."

"Stay out of this, Ray. I swore I'd get the bastard that killed Otto Finney, and by God, I'm going to do it." He stepped in front of me and shoved the watch in my face. "It's yours, isn't it? You admit it?"

"I told you it was mine." My heart sank. I could feel the ground falling out from under me.

"Ah right, now I'll tell you where we found your watch. Just about an hour ago we picked it up near the railroad tracks where Bunt Manley was murdered. See this leather strap? The stitching is rotten. That's how you lost the watch. You killed Manley, probably while he was here at the station, then you put him in his own car and put the car on the tracks to make it look like an accident. But while you were fooling with that car you caught your watch strap on something and the stitching pulled loose and you lost it. That's the way it happened, isn't it?"

That was exactly the way it happened. But the first shock had worn off and now I was more angry than afraid. I said, "Otis, that's the craziest story I ever heard of. Are you actually accusing me of killing somebody?"

"I'm not accusing you, I'm telling you!"

I turned to the deputy. "Ray, for God's sake, what's got into him? Has he gone out of his mind completely?"

Ray only looked at me. This was Otis Miller's play and he wasn't going to try to take it from him. I wheeled back to the Sheriff.

"Tell me one thing," I said, "just one thing, before you make any more of these crazy accusations. Why in the world would I want to kill Bunt Manley when I hardly even knew the man?"

"Maybe you didn't want to kill him," the Sheriff spat. "But maybe you had to kill him. Maybe he came around wanting a bigger share of the money and you decided you had to kill him."

"What money are you talking about? This gets crazier all the time!"

"You know what money, Hooper. The same money you and Bunt Manley took from old Provo's box factory. If I have to spell it out for you, by God, I'll do it. I've been keeping my eye on Manley ever since he got out of the pen. He's never been any good and I knew sooner or later he'd get himself in bad trouble. So Manley was the one I thought of first when you broke into the factory and killed the old watchman. But Manley couldn't have done the job alone. Somebody had to be in it with him, so when I started looking for a partner I found you."

The Sheriffs voice was still, soft, and sure.

I was practically yelling. "What the hell do you mean? I thought you were a responsible man, Otis, but here you are building a case on nothing but thin air and making these insane accusations! Well, I've had enough of it! I demand that you offer some proof or shut up and get out of here!"

He grinned. "That suits me fine. We'll start with that bogus bill that you brought around to my office right after the robbery. I knew at the time you were lying through your teeth about just getting it, because that kind of paper hasn't been seen in more than a year. That was a mistake, Hooper, because I started to wonder why you'd go to that much trouble to pump me about the robbery."

I snorted. "I didn't pump you. I might have mentioned it casually. Hell, the whole town was talking about it. If I mentioned it, do you call that proof that I had a hand in it or killed Manley?"

"And Otto Finney, too," he said softly. "Don't forget Otto. No, it doesn't prove anything in particular, but it all adds up to a jury."

We stood there glaring at each other and nobody had to tell me that he had me by the throat and I was fighting for my life. From here on out it would be brass knucks, and I knew it. I tried to get set for it.

"All right," he said, and his voice was hard now, hitting like a hammer. "Here's something maybe you didn't know. We knew Manley got some ideas during his stay in Leavenworth. We figured he'd try something like this before long. But Manley was smart, we didn't learn a thing from him, so we figured our best bet was to find the man who was in it with him. That turned out to be easier than I had hoped, when we found Otto's body in the lake with that flywheel tied to him. That was your big mistake, Hooper, that flywheel."

It wasn't "Joe" now, it was "Hooper," and he said it as though he had a mouthful of quinine.

"That flywheel is the thing that cooked you, Hooper. We have Ike Abrams' word that he took it out of your father's car and left it in the back of your station. No mistake about it, it's the same flywheel. The jury will take Ike's word for that. You and Bunt Manley robbed the box factory and killed the watchman; then you smeared Otto's fingerprints all over the safe to throw me off the track. Finally you brought the body out here, weighted it with that flywheel, then took it out to the lake and dumped it. It's as simple as that and I can prove every damn word of it.

"Have you heard enough? Well, I'm not through yet. There's plenty more. There's something else that started me thinking about you, Hooper. That visit of yours to the box factory. You hadn't been near that factory for years, not since you used to work there, but on the day before the robbery you made the trip just to pay a five-dollar debt. I ask you, does a story like that hold water? Like hell it does! You went out there to get the exact layout in your mind because the robbery was all set for the next night, when you knew the entire payroll would be in the safe. You prowled around the front office, where the safe was, then you went back to the warehouse and talked to some of the workmen."

I was almost ready to explode. "All this talk doesn't prove a damn thing and you know it!"

Otis grinned tightly. "It proves plenty, and I can see your guts crawling. Do you know how long the factory burglar alarm had been installed, Hooper? Just two days! That means that whoever took the money and killed the watchman gave that place a thorough going-over not more than two days before the job. And you're the man, Hooper. I can put my hands on at least twenty people who will testify to it. How does it look to you now, Hooper? The jury will throw the book at you. When the story gets out, you'll be lucky if they don't lynch you on the courthouse lawn."

My voice deserted me. I couldn't make a sound.

"I'm not making any promises, Hooper, but if you'll sign a statement I'll at least see that you get a fair trial."

My brain was numb. I just stood there too sick to move.

Then a light stabbed the darkness outside the cabin, and I heard the sound of my father's old Dodge pulling up in front of my door.

Ray King said, "It's your father, I think, Joe."

"Look," I said. "Don't say anything to him about this. Not now, anyway. He has a patient next door. That's the only reason he's out here."

Otis Miller said nothing. The two of them looked at each other and finally Ray nodded. I went to the door and said, "Dad, is that you?"

"Yes, Joe. It's pretty late for you to be up, isn't it?"

"Some friends of mine dropped in. Anyway, I wanted to stay

up till you got here. I don't know how important it is, but his wife seems to think he's getting worse."

I could see him standing there, a stooped, bone-tired old man. After a moment he turned and walked heavily toward Number 2.

"How about it, Hooper?" Otis said. "You ready to sign that statement?"

The brief escape from the Sheriffs hammering had given me a chance to get things straight in my mind. At first I felt empty and helpless. I knew they had me. There was absolutely no doubt about it, and I might as well do what they said. So this is the way it ends, Hooper.

After a moment I turned to the Sheriff and looked dully into those eyes of his.

That was the thing that saved me.

I had expected to see the iron-hard glint of victory in those eyes. But it wasn't there. There was anticipation, anxiety, expectation, but not that glint of complete victory. At last I recognized what I saw there. Otis Miller's eyes were the eyes of a gambler who had just run an outrageous bluff and was waiting for his opponent to call.

The implication struck me like an icy shower. It jarred me awake, it released the numbness in my brain. Otis Miller didn't have a damn thing on me! Maybe he had tried to run the most fantastic bluff in history, but he still didn't have a leg to stand on and he knew it.

Oh, he knew I was guilty, all right. He was mixed up about Manley, but he had me pegged every inch of the way. But he couldn't prove a bit of it. All that loud talk of his had been so much hogwash in the hope that he could panic me into a confession.

I felt like a teen-ager on his first drunk. I wanted to laugh right in Otis Miller's face and then kick him and Ray King out of my cabin. What I did was look at Otis and grin.

"Now," I said, "are you through, Otis?" The glee of the top dog was bubbling inside me. "Are you finally through shooting off that fat mouth of yours? Because if you are, I've got a few things to say that might interest you."

He reacted just the way I had known he would, as though I had whipped him across the face with a pistol butt.

I had to laugh then; I couldn't hold it back. "Who the hell do you think you are, Otis? None of your talk means a thing. That flywheel story, for instance. There's no way in the world you can prove the flywheel was in my station on the night of the robbery. It was hauled away to the dumping grounds almost a month before, where anybody could have picked it up. As for the bogus bill, I always thought it was a sheriff's duty to take care of things like that. You can suspect anything you please, Otis, but you'd better be damn sure you have proof to back you up before you accuse people of robbery and murder."

He opened his mouth but I didn't give him a chance to say a word.

"That visit to the factory," I said. "No jury is going to convict a man for going out of his way to pay an honest debt. That burglar alarm doesn't prove a thing, either, because any top law officer will tell you that any burglar worth his salt takes care of burglar alarms as a matter of course. That just about blows your conviction sky-high, doesn't it, Otis?"

I wasn't through yet. When you got Otis down, it was a good idea to kick him, just to be safe.

"What else is there?" I said. "Oh, yes, the watch. Well, listen carefully, Otis, because this is what happened to my watch. I missed it tonight just before Bunt Manley drove up for gas. I figured at the time the strap had broken and I'd dropped it somewhere, and I intended to look for it when I wasn't busy. While Manley was here I saw him pick something up, but I didn't think anything about it at the time. Manley wouldn't be above picking up a watch, of course, but I didn't think about that until it was too late. So that's what happened to my watch. Also, while Manley was here I noticed that he had been drinking and mentioned that he shouldn't be driving in his condition, but he wouldn't listen to me. Half drunk, he stalled his car on the railroad tracks and got himself killed by a train. Later, you found my watch near the scene of the accident, which isn't surprising. I'll bet you found a lot of other things, too, didn't you, Otis, scattered clear to hell and gone, probably?"

I had shown the cape to the bull but he hadn't charged. He got red in the face, his throat swelled, veins stood out on his forehead, but he didn't charge because he knew that he couldn't win. Ray King stood stiffly, looking grim, but Otis was almost crazy with rage and frustration. Maybe a full minute went by before he made a sound, before he trusted himself to open his mouth.

Suddenly he wheeled and went to the door, then he turned and came back. "You think you're smart, don't you, Hooper? Well, listen to me."

"You listen to *me!*" I said. "If you think you've got something, you're welcome to use it. Take me down to the courthouse, lock me up, bring me to trial. You try that, Otis, and you'll be the laughingstock of the country. The jury wouldn't be out thirty seconds before they come in with a verdict of not guilty."

That was the reason I was so sure that nothing was going to happen. Otis wasn't going to bring me in until he had the evidence he needed, and he didn't have it. The law of double jeopardy worked in Creston as well as it did in other places, and once they found me not guilty it would be over, no matter what Otis might turn up later.

Ray King touched his boss's arm. "Well, Otis?"

I could see the angry blood pumping in the Sheriffs throat, but he took a tight rein on his voice. "You're guilty, Hooper," he said softly. "You're guilty as hell and I won't let up on you until I see you cooked. You can bank on it!"

Then he tramped out, stiffly, like a mechanical man operating on overwound springs. Even the back of his neck looked angry as he went out.

I stood at the door as the two men got in the car, circled the cabin, and headed toward the highway.

Well, I had won that round, but he was a bulldog, that Otis Miller. He had his teeth in my throat and he wasn't going to turn loose until I was dead. There was only one answer—I had to get out of Creston, far away from Creston, before he scraped together a real case against me.

I heard the door slam at the Sheldon cabin, and when I looked out the window I saw my dad heading for his car. I went to the door and started to speak, but he didn't even look in my direction. He leaned against the car for a moment. Then he looked up at the white clouds sliding under the pale belly of the moon and I thought I heard him say something, but I couldn't catch what it was. Finally he got into his car and drove away.

I kicked the door open and headed for Number 2.

I ran into Paula at the door of the Sheldon cabin; she was just coming out. "Joe," she said quickly, "I'm afraid we're in trouble."

"You can say that again. Do you know who I've been fighting with for the past half hour? The Sheriff!"

"At this time of night!"

"The time of day or night doesn't mean a thing to Otis Miller. Didn't you hear the car?"

"I heard it, but I thought it was your father. I thought he had stopped to talk to you before looking at Karl."

"It was the Sheriff, all right, and he threw the book at me. He hit me with everything he could get his hands on. Luckily, it wasn't enough to panic me into a confession, the way he had hoped."

Her eyes widened. "Do you mean he actually suspects you of that robbery?"

"He doesn't suspect, he *knows*. There's absolutely no doubt about it in his mind. But he doesn't have the evidence to convince a jury, and that's the only thing that saved me. Paula, we've got to get out of here, and we've got to do it in a hurry!" I went inside, dropped on a chair, and looked at Sheldon, who seemed to be asleep. "What did Dad say about him?" I asked.

"He has a high fever, but he should be all right tomorrow. We'll leave tomorrow night."

I was too tired to argue. Anyway, I needed some rest. All of us did, before starting the trip to Arkansas. Then I remembered something. "You said something about trouble," I said, looking up at her. "What is it?"

"Your father. He knows everything."

I felt the nervous tingling of my scalp. "The factory, the killing? How could he know?"

"He saw those sketches you made for Karl. I had meant to burn them, but so much has happened.... Anyway, he saw them, and the minute he looked at them he knew everything."

A cold void opened in my bowels. This was the beginning of a sickness that I knew would never be cured. Paula sat on the arm of the chair, then put her hands on my shoulders and gently massaged the back of my neck. "He can just guess," I said. "He doesn't really know." "He knows," she said, "because

I told him. I thought if I laid it on the line for him, it would scare him so that he wouldn't dare go to the police. Now I don't know."

"What do you mean?"

"Your father has a conscience," she said. "A strong one. It will eat at him until he'll finally have to do something about it."

I got out of the chair so suddenly that I almost knocked her off the arm. I went to the door and looked out at the darkness, remembering how he had looked standing there beside his car, his face turned up to the black sky. Paula came over and stood beside me.

"What are we going to do, Joe?"

"What can we do?"

Her voice was suddenly brittle, and it was one of those rare times when I felt that she actually understood what it was to be afraid. "Don't you understand?" she said. "He knows everything! Sooner or later—maybe not tomorrow or the next day, but pretty soon—he won't be able to hold it inside him. He'll start talking and he'll tell everything he knows."

"By that time we'll be far away from Creston."

"That won't help us. For murder, they'll come after you, no matter where you are."

"All right," I said tightly, "you think of something. It was your idea to tell him everything."

She said nothing. She just stood there beside me looking out at the night. But somehow I knew what she was thinking. I knew her well enough to guess the solution that would come instinctively to her mind. I took one of her arms and jerked her around to face me.

"You can forget it!" I said. "You can damn well forget it right now!"

There was a flicker of pain in her eyes. "Joe, I don't know what you're talking about."

"You know, all right!" I let her go and she almost fell.

There was nothing—absolutely nothing—that she wouldn't do. She would have killed my father in a minute, because he had become dangerous to her. Several long seconds passed as we stood there staring at each other, as we sized each other up like two savages. Then she closed her eyes, swayed, and leaned against me. Those arms of hers went around my neck and her face tilted up to mine.

"I'm sorry, Joe. You can see right through me, can't you? You can read me like a book."

I said nothing.

"I'm over it now," she said huskily. "Things will work out fine. You'll see."

## Chapter Seventeen

The first thing I did the next morning was write a letter.

Dad:

I guess you knew this would happen sooner or later. The station and tourist-court business just didn't work out. Everything seems to have gone to pieces this past year—first the business, then breaking up with Beth. There's no reason why I should stay on in Creston, so I'm pulling out. The bank can take over the station, if they want it. They would have done it anyway in another month or so....

I wrote the letter for the jury's benefit, in case I ever had to face a jury. At least they couldn't say I was running away without a legitimate reason. When I finished the letter I went to the station and opened up as usual.

It was a long day, that day. I kept telling myself that in a few hours Creston and all its memories would be behind me, and Paula and I would start building something for ourselves. I never thought about our future, just the beginning of it.

The end I didn't want to know.

I wasn't afraid of my father's telling what he knew. After all, I was his son, and a man doesn't go out of his way to send his son to the electric chair. I actually hated Paula every time I thought of her telling him everything. The hate became so powerful at times that my hands ached to get around that pale, soft throat of hers—but I knew what would happen if I tried it. She would look at me and I would be kissing her.

The best thing to do was forget it. My father was hurt and there was no way to ease the pain. And there was no changing the way I felt about Paula, either. Forget it.

I tried. I cleaned all around the grease rack and straightened things in back of the station, and somehow the morning became afternoon and after a long while Ike came, as he always did.

"How's it goin', Joe?"

"All right, I guess. You take over for a while. I think I'll go back to the shack and wash up a little."

"Sure."

Ike thought I was acting strange, and I guess I was. But every hour now seemed like a year, and I kept looking at my wrist for the watch that wasn't there. Every time I did it I thought of Otis Miller and wondered if he and Ray King had dug up anything else or if they would be back to take up the questioning again.

They didn't come back. Maybe they had somebody watching me, but I doubted it. So I went to my cabin, took a cold shower, and gave myself a few minutes to settle down, and then I began packing. I threw all my clothes into suitcases, rounded up a few other things I would need, like toilet articles and razor blades, and not until that minute did I remember the gun. That revolver that Sheldon had given me. The one that had killed Otto Finney.

I didn't want to keep it on me, but I sure couldn't leave it here in my cabin. Finally I shoved it into my waistband, under my shirt. It felt cold and deadly, like a coiled snake.

It was almost sundown when I left my cabin. Ike was doing something in front of the station but he didn't seem to be looking my way, so I went over to the Sheldons'. Paula and her husband were having what sounded like a serious talk when I came in, but they broke it off and Paula stood up.

"Are you ready, Joe?"

"I was ready days ago." I looked at Sheldon. "How do you feel?"

"Better than I did yesterday. Have you heard any more from the Sheriff?"

"No, but that doesn't mean he's stopped working on me." I turned to Paula. "You've got everything ready to go, haven't you? I want to pull out as soon as it's time to close the station. With a little luck we ought to be well into Arkansas by sunup tomorrow."

"Everything's ready," she said. "But I want your father to have another look at Karl before we leave."

I stared at her. "Are you crazy? We've pushed my father just about as far as he'll go. It simply won't do to have him come again."

"Would you like it better if Karl's arm became infected again, and we had to go to another doctor somewhere? A doctor we didn't know?" She turned suddenly, went to the window, and stood looking flatly at the sleazy curtains. "It doesn't seem very smart to me," she said. "The answer is no," I said.

"All right. But it seems like a little thing to fight about. If your father just brought out some sulfa, we'd have nothing to worry about. We wouldn't have to depend on doctors."

"No."

But I was weakening, and she could tell it. She turned from the window and said, "I know what's worrying you. You just don't want to see him, do you? Well, you won't have to. I can drive into town and pick up the drugs and dressings we'll need; all you have to do is let him know I'm coming."

It seemed a little thing. It didn't seem possible that it could cause my father any more pain. After a moment I said, "It's no good. You don't even know where the house is."

"I can find it. I've been in bigger towns than Creston. All you have to do is give me the directions."

What a hell of a fuss about nothing! I thought. It was beginning to grate on my nerves. "All right!" I said finally. "If it will make you happy, you can drive in and get the medicine you need. I guess it's all right."

"Of course it's all right," she said. "The Sheriff doesn't suspect me and Karl. If I should be seen, it wouldn't mean anything."

"I know all that, and I said it was all right!" I was getting jumpy, much too jumpy. I just wanted to get away from here—far away. That was the only thing I could think of. I walked to the door and said, "I think I'll go to the station."

Sheldon said, "You'd better send your helper home and close the station yourself when the time comes." I nodded and went out.

Darkness had settled over that bald Oklahoma prairie, but it was still early and there was plenty of traffic on the highway. As I came around to the front of the station I saw that Ike had washed down the cement driveway by the gas pumps, and now he was spraying water around the station to settle the dust.

I didn't know just what to do about Ike. We were friends

and he had been a lot of help to me with the station, and I didn't feel like picking up and leaving him without a word. He turned and grinned when he heard me come up.

"Hot as hell tonight."

"Yeah." I went inside and checked the cash register. I took out enough to cover Ike's salary for two weeks and it just about cleaned it out. "Ike," I called, "can you come here a minute?"

"Sure." He hung up the water hose and came inside. I handed him the money.

"What's this, Joe?"

"Two week's pay, Ike. It looks like you're out of a job."

He looked as though he had been slapped. "You mean I'm fired, Joe?"

"I mean the business is on the rocks. You know as well as I do that we've barely made expenses these past few months, if that."

He stood there for a moment, looking stupid. He scratched his head. "You mean you're throwin' it up, Joe? You're quittin'?"

"There's nothing left to do. If you can't make this kind of business pay during the tourist season, then you might as well give up."

He looked uncomfortable as he took the money, folded it slowly, and put it in his pocket. "By golly, Joe, I'm sorry to hear it. I kind of liked working out here. You've been a good boss."

"Thanks, Ike."

"If there's anything I can do..."

"Just one thing, Ike." I counted out forty dollars, most of it from my pocket. "This is what I owe the gas company on the last delivery. Will you contact them tomorrow and pay them off?"

His forehead wrinkled at that one. "Ike," I said, "I'm just sick of this place. When I close up tonight I don't want to have to look at it or think about it again. Maybe I'll just pack up and go fishing or something. Anyway, I'd appreciate it if you'd take care of the gasoline people."

"Well, sure, Joe, if that's the way you want it. I guess I know how you feel. The business has been pretty much of a disappointment, at that, I guess."

"Ike," I said, "that's the understatement of the year."

I had expected something of a fuss, or at least a pep talk, for Ike was a great one for seeing a thing through to the end. But he was surprisingly calm, as though he had seen it coming from a long way off—and maybe he had.

"Well, Joe..."

"I guess that's it, Ike."

We said a few more things, none of them making much sense, and finally I got Ike in his Ford and headed him for town.

The last small thread was cut. I was free. Automatically, I began locking up, bringing in the display cases of oil, disconnecting the water hose, locking the pumps. I looked out at the highway and thought: I'm free! Free to go anywhere I damn please!

Far up the highway I could see the lights atop the towering grain elevators. Creston, Oklahoma. If I never saw it again, it would be fine with me.

Just as I finished locking up I heard Paula starting the Buick. She drove around to the front of the station. I went around to the driver's side of the car and thought: Christ, she can be beautiful when she wants to! I'll never forget how she looked at that moment as she reached through the window and traced her fingers lightly over my chest.

"It won't be long now, Joe. Within another hour this town will be behind us."

"I'm ready."

"We'll start just as soon as I get back. Just as soon as I pick up the medicine and dressings from your father. You didn't forget to call him, did you?"

"I didn't have a chance. Ike left just a few minutes ago. But I'll do it now, if you're still sure it's necessary."

"I explained it to you, Joe. It's insurance we've got to have. If Karl's arm should get bad again, we won't find another doctor as co-operative as your father."

I still didn't like it, but when Paula got hold of something she wouldn't turn it loose without a fight. And right now I didn't feel like a fight. "All right," I said finally, "I guess you'll have it your way."

I had to unlock the station again to get to the phone. I got the number and listened to the ringing at the other end, and at last a thousand-year-old voice, a voice without life, said, "Hello."

"Dad, this is Joe. I've got a little favor to ask of you."

He didn't say a thing. For a moment I thought he had hung

up on me, but then I heard the hum of the open line and knew that he was still there.

"Dad, this is the last thing I'm going to ask of you. Believe me, it is. You know this man you've been treating; well, he and his wife are pulling out tonight. They're pulling out for good and you'll never hear of them again. But the woman wants you to give her some medicine, just in case her husband's arm starts acting up again. I'm sending her over to pick it up. Is that all right?"

There was only the hum of the wire.

"Dad, are you still there?"

"Yes."

"You'll let her have the medicine, won't you? Sulfa, or whatever you think best."

"Do I have a choice, Joe?"

I felt like hell. For a moment I just stood there with the receiver in my hand, unable to think of anything else to say, and finally I hung up.

I went outside, where Paula was waiting. "It's all right," I said. "But make it fast. Don't drag it out any longer than is absolutely necessary. I'm afraid he's had just about all he can take."

I told her how to get to the house, which wasn't much of a job. The town wasn't big enough to get lost in, and anyway, the streets were clearly marked. She smiled faintly and squeezed my hand, then she put the Buick in gear and left me standing there. God, I thought, I'll be glad when it's over!

After I got the station locked again, I went around to Number 2 to see how Sheldon was doing. He was doing fine. He had his clothes on and was doing some packing as I came in.

"You're looking pretty good," I said.

He looked at me, then looked away, fast. "I'll feel better when we're away from here."

"Well, it shouldn't be long now. It won't take Paula long to pick up the medicine."

He wouldn't look at me. He kept fiddling with a shirt that he was trying to get folded, keeping me behind him. He looked nervous and pale, but I put that down to his sickness.

I said, "You want me to help you with that?"

"No!" He turned on me then, and there was something in

those eyes of his that put ice in my veins. "What's the matter with you?" I said. "Nothing! Just get out of here and leave me alone! Do you have to stand there watching me, watching every move I make?"

"Look," I said, "you're pretty jumpy, aren't you? Hadn't you better just sit down and take it easy?"

I thought for a minute that he was going to spring at me. Then he seemed to go to mush inside. He leaned against the bed, then he sat down and put his face in his hands. I guess that was when the first germ of fear became implanted in my brain. I looked at Sheldon and knew that something was wrong, something was wrong as hell. Here he had just pulled through a serious sickness and within an hour would be on his way to freedom, and he looked like a man getting ready to walk his last mile. I stepped over to him, pushed his head back, and made him look at me.

"What's eating you, Sheldon?"

"Nothing."

"Oh, yes, there is! Something's got its fangs in your guts and I want to know what it is."

"I tell you it's nothing!"

I think I already knew. In the dark cellar of my mind I knew what it was. Panic's cold feet raced up my spine as I grabbed the front of Sheldon's shirt. I heard myself saying it, before the thought was really clear in my mind.

"Out with it, Sheldon! Does it have anything to do with my father?"

He whined, and I slammed him across the face with the back of my fist.

"Goddamn you, you'd better tell it and tell it fast, or you're going to curse the day you were born! Has it got anything to do with my father?"

But he was too sick and too scared and too weak to make a sound. I hit him again, knowing it was hopeless, knowing that it was a waste of time, but I hit him. His mouth came open and his teeth were red with blood.

"It's Paula, isn't it?" I almost yelled at him. "What's she going to do? What's she got in that hard little brain of hers?"

But I already knew. It was in Sheldon's eyes, gleaming there in the twin small seas of pain. Paula was going to kill my father.

He knew too much about her, so she was going to kill him.

I should have guessed. I should have known when I first saw that look in her eyes the night before. That was when she had made up her mind.

I felt sick. All day she had been planning it. She had made up that story about having to go after medicine, knowing that I wouldn't have the guts to face my father myself, now that he knew all about us. She was going to murder him. Right this minute she was on her way. '

It seemed like a lifetime as I stood there, my fist doubled, ready to hit Sheldon again. I thought: She must have known that I'd find out. She couldn't keep a thing like this a secret. How she meant to explain it to me, I couldn't guess—but she would think of something. I knew her well enough for that. With the help of that ripe mouth and soft body she would think of something, and make it sound logical enough, when the time came.

But the time would not come. I was almost sorry as I thought it. The end had already arrived.

I let Sheldon go and he fell to the floor, still whimpering. I could have killed him without a qualm, as easily as stepping on a spider, but there was no time for it. I was out of the cabin and racing through the night toward my car.

I drove like a crazy man, deaf and dumb, blind to everything but the grayish highway and the dazzling lights that rushed at me from the darkness and then fell swiftly behind. I assaulted the night with speed, split it open and made it scream. Past the floodlighted oil-field supply houses, the wind rushing. Past the big motels and the crumby shacks. Past the towering grain elevators; pale, unbelievable giants in the darkness, topped with blinking red lights. Over the railroad overpass and down the breath-taking slope on the other side to Creston.

How I got there, I didn't know. But I was there. I had not passed the Buick—that was one thing I was sure of—and that meant that Paula had reached Creston before me. I drove as though each second were a matter of life or death. And it was. I skirted the heart of town to avoid traffic. Maybe, just maybe...

The tires screamed as I took a corner too fast, too sharp. There was a spine-shattering jar as the front wheel hit the curb.

The explosion blew a ragged hole in the night, in my hopes. The right front tire went out and the Chevy careened sideways, jumped the curb, crashed into a squat cement marker, and came to a shuddering halt.

The starter wouldn't work. I jabbed it and there was nothing but silence. Up and down the street doors came open, people came out to see what the noise was about. The car wouldn't start. Maybe it was a battery cable broken loose, maybe it was something else. Whatever it was, I didn't have time to look into it. I got out of the car and began running.

People were pouring into the street. I ignored their shouted questions. I ran.

Through alleys, up streets, across yards, over hedges I ran. From one end of town to the other, almost, I ran, with fire in my lungs and ice in my belly. I almost forgot why I was running. The muscles in my thighs quivered, my knees wanted to buckle. Just a minute, I thought. Rest just a minute. Give yourself a chance to breathe. And then I would remember and keep going.

The Buick was the first thing I saw. I passed the church and the Langford house, and then I wiped the sweat from my eyes and there was the blue Buick parked at the curb in front of my father's house. How long it had been there, I didn't know. But not too long. Paula would have taken it easy on a strange street in a strange town. She couldn't have driven so very fast. Whether or not it had been fast enough, only time would tell.

I almost fell on my face when I reached the car. I couldn't get enough air into my lungs, no matter how hard I tried. Then I saw that the car was empty, and that gave me a new strength. I staggered like a drunk man, a straw man, an empty shell of a man. I shoved the front gate open and stumbled up the walk to the front porch. The porch light was on. The front door was open, because of the heat, and there was a light in the front room. There was also a light on the south side of the house, in my father's bedroom. I noticed all this as I stumbled toward the porch. And then I saw Paula.

She was standing almost in the center of the front room, calm and erect, with no flicker of emotion on her beautiful face. In her hand was Sheldon's .38 revolver and it was pointed at the door of my father's bedroom.

An ocean of hopelessness washed over me. I was too late.

I wanted to let go and sink to the bottom depths and never look up again.

And then I heard my father calling, his voice muffled, "Just a minute. I'll be with you in just a minute."

Thank God! My heart took up its beating again, and now I could see the situation as it was. My father had been napping, probably—about the only kind of sleep he got. Obviously, Paula had got here just ahead of me. She had stepped into the front room and called out, and now...

And now the nightmare was reality. My father would open the bedroom door. Perhaps he would get one startled look at Paula and the gun, and then he would be dead. Panic and exhaustion held me frozen. I tried to call out to Paula, and no sound came from my throat.

The door to my father's bedroom opened. He stood framed in the doorway, wearing a faded blue bathrobe and ragged carpet slippers. His thin hair was tousled, his eyes swollen with sleep, and I don't think he even saw Paula's gun before the sudden blast cracked the night.

I stood there, my throat swollen with a yell that would not come out. My father did not fall. Startled, he jerked to one side. With wide, unbelieving eyes, he stared at Paula as she took one step toward him, then another....

Slowly, languidly, gracefully—almost beautifully—she died.

She seemed almost to melt to the floor. There was hardly a sound as Paula went down to her knees, and then she fell over on her shoulder and lay staring blankly at the front wall of the room. The thing I noticed was how cold and beautiful she looked. Her mouth seemed brazenly red.

Not until later did I realize that I had taken my own .38 from my waistband, and that the barrel was hot, and that a whisper of burned powder had become mingled with the clean smell of the summer night. Perhaps several seconds went by before I realized fully that Paula was dead and that I had killed her.

There seemed nothing to do after that. Nothing I wanted to do.

I sat on the front porch and held my face in my hands, and after a while the Sheriff came.

## Chapter Eighteen

The wall clock in the Sheriff's office said seven o'clock. We had been there almost eight hours, Otis, Ray King, and a county stenographer taking down everything I said. The Sheriff didn't know it, but he was doing me a favor by keeping me there. I didn't want to be left alone. Every time I closed my eyes I saw Paula. I could imagine what it would be like if I tried to sleep. A great numbness had taken hold of me now, and that was the way I wanted to keep it. I was a hollow man, without feelings, without conscience, with sensibilities, but I knew that wouldn't last if they left me to myself.

Otis Miller, his thick face beginning to sag with weariness, sat staring at me with red-rimmed eyes. Unbelieving eyes. He had known me all my life, I guess. Doc Hooper's boy. Tackle on the high-school football team, soldiered with a tank outfit in Africa and France. A little erratic, maybe, but would settle down eventually and marry Steve Langford's girl. That was the way he'd had me pegged, more than likely, before the robbery. He was trying to figure out what would make a boy like that turn to robbing and killing.

He wasn't having much luck. Fatigue had dulled the edge of his imagination. He had all the facts before him— I had given them to him, almost gladly—but they were just the bare facts and didn't tell the whole story.

I was guilty, all right. There was no doubt in the Sheriff's mind about that. It was the *why* of the thing that stumped him.

"All right, Hooper," he said heavily, "let's hear it again."

He wasn't giving up yet, and I was glad of that. I wanted to keep talking, I wanted to have people around me. That was the important thing. I just didn't want to be taken to a cell and left to myself.

"All right, Otis. What do you want to know?" My voice sounded lifeless. I felt lifeless and hollow. It was a strange, cold feeling.

"First," the Sheriff said, "let's get the main facts straight again. Is it true that on the night of the fourteenth you and this Karl Sheldon robbed Max Provo's box factory?"

"It's true."

Like a wooden dummy talking.

"And on that same night you killed old Otto Finney and disposed of the body in the lake?"

"True."

A wooden dummy. You put your hand inside the hollow dummy, and you press on something, and its mouth comes open and it seems to talk. That was the way it seemed to me. The words just came out and I had nothing to do with them at all.

"Who helped you dispose of the body?"

Something went wrong with the dummy. The mouth came open but the words wouldn't come out. I couldn't make myself say Paula's name.

"The woman?" the Sheriff said. "The Sheldon woman?"

I nodded.

"Then what happened?"

"That's about all. We split the money and they went away."

"Where did they go?"

"Somewhere in Texas, I think."

"All right. We have all the details about Bunt Manley and the Sheldon woman. You killed them, too; is that right?"

I nodded.

"The stenographer has it all down. Do you have anything to add to your original statement concerning the deaths of Manley and the Sheldon woman?"

"I guess not."

He turned to the stenographer. "For the record, you'd better put in that this confession was not obtained through duress or force. Is that right, Hooper?"

"Yes, that's right."

"Do you have anything else to add to the statement before it's typed up?"

At some point during the night Otis had dropped his toughness. He was almost gentle now. "Do you want to talk to a lawyer before signing the statement?"

Sheldon was still alive and would talk his head off, and I

knew it. I said, "A lawyer couldn't help me."

Otis gave the signal and the stenographer gathered up his notes and left the room. The Sheriff and his deputy sat there staring at me.

It was all over. Otis said, "Well, Hooper, we might as well go over to the jail."

For the first time in eight hours a real emotion went to work on me. Fear. Fear of being put in a cell and left to, myself.

Ray King said, "Is there something else you want to say?"

Suddenly I felt an insane urge to laugh. "We almost got away with it." I heard myself saying. "We came so close!"

"You're wrong, Hooper," the Sheriff said. "You couldn't be more wrong if you tried." Suddenly he pushed himself back from his desk, still not satisfied with the bare facts. He still wanted an answer, but he wasn't sure of the question. He said, "You never had a chance, Hooper. We're not completely stupid down here. We had you nailed to that box-factory job and, in spite of what you think, we could have made a good case in court. But we also knew you didn't pull the robbery alone. I figured Bunt Manley helped you, but I was wrong in that. Anyway, we didn't want to pull you in until we found out who was in it with you. With all the circumstantial evidence we had on you, do you think we'd just forget about you?"

He snorted. "We had you watched day and night, Hooper. Ike Abrams or one of my deputies reported every move you made. You thought you were going to leave this town scot-free, didn't you? Well, let me tell you, you couldn't have got away in a Patton tank. We were just waiting for you or the Sheldons to make a mistake, and when you did make one it was a lulu!"

I stared at him. "You had Ike spying on me all the time?"

"You're a murderer, Hooper. Ike was doing a job for the Sheriff's office. And it didn't take him long to tie you up with Sheldon's wife. After that it was just a matter of waiting. There's one thing I'm curious about though. Why did you kill her?"

I closed my eyes and there she was.

I could almost feel sorry for Sheldon; he wouldn't die easy in the chair. Maybe I wouldn't, either, but the prospect was not frightening now. I had died the instant my finger had pulled the trigger on that .38. With a woman like Paula it seemed ridiculous to think such thoughts—but I had loved her. I must have loved her to have done the things I had done.

Ray King said, "Maybe I'll never understand it, Joe, but I'd like to try. You threw over a fine girl like Beth Langford, then turned to robbing and murdering because of a woman like Paula Sheldon. Why?"

I thought of the cell that was waiting for me. When I reached it I wanted to be able to drop into dreamless, thoughtless oblivion—and the time was not yet.

I looked at them and they were waiting for the answer. They wanted a simple, clear-cut answer and there wasn't any.

It was a long story. Almost a month ago, I thought; that was when I saw her for the first time. That was when the Buick stopped on the highway in front of the station. Less than a month ago it had been. It seemed like a thousand lifetimes.

Otis and Ray were waiting and I didn't know where to begin. And then I thought dully: Begin at the beginning, and maybe there will be an answer there for you, as well as for them. And I said:

"This is the way it was...." And I started at the beginning.

Printed in the USA
CPSIA information can be obtained
at www.ICGtesting.com
LVHW041613140823
755203LV00012B/234